THE RHEA JENSEN SERIES

BOOK 3

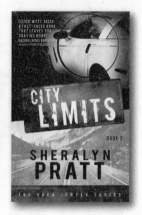

THE RHEA JENSEN SERIES

BOOK 3

SHERALYN PRATT

BONNEVILLE BOOKS
SPRINGVILLE, UTAH

© 2010 Sheralyn Pratt

ISBN 13: 978-1-59955-423-5

Published by Bonneville Books, an imprint of Cedar Fort, Inc., 2373 W. 700 S., Springville, UT 84663
Distributed by Cedar Fort, Inc., www.cedarfort.com

LIBRARY OF CONGRESS CATALOGING-IN-PUBLICATION DATA

Pratt, Sheralyn.
  city limits / Sheralyn Pratt.
    p. cm.
  Originally published: Salt Lake City, Utah : Spectrum Books, c2003.
  ISBN 978-1-59955-423-5 (alk. paper)
  1. Women private investigators—Fiction. 2. Embezzlement—Fiction. 3. Mormon missionaries—Fiction. I. Title.

  PS3616.R3846S67 2010
  813'.6—dc22

  2010005457

Cover design by Angela D. Olsen
Cover design © 2010 by Lyle Mortimer
Edited and typeset by Megan E. Welton

Printed in the United States of America

10 9 8 7 6 5 4 3 2 1

To Angela—it's about time someone dedicated a book to you. Thanks for rocking the covers and everything else!

ACKNOWLEDGMENTS

As always, thanks to great editors: Megan, Kimiko, and Melissa. I'd be nowhere with out all the people who make their friends read the book. Thanks to my mom, who likes having an author for a daughter, and to Cedar Fort for believing in my writing.

ONE

WHOEVER HE WAS, the man was a scoot from death. He sat with both legs dangling ten stories above street level, his hands gripping the ledge and pushing his body into a precarious forward lean. A hundred feet below, a large crowd gathered to witness the potential suicide of a man whose name no one knew.

"He's not going to do it," Kay said in a puff of frustration. She took one last look in her pocket mirror and returned it to her purse as her cameraman looked up from adjusting his tripod to see if he had heard her correctly.

Looking up from some law enforcement profiles on my laptop, I gazed across the expanse between our roof and the jumper's ledge and agreed with her. The body language was all wrong. The man might be leaning forward, but he was also seated as close to his hotel window as possible. His face was free of tension and he actually appeared impatient. Or maybe I just got that impression after the third time he checked his watch in ten minutes. He looked more like a man waiting for a late bus than a man on the cusp of death—from our vantage point at least, which happened to be the perfect filming location.

Too perfect?

My eyes moved up and down the neighboring hotel,

wondering why the jumper chose that particular floor to jump from and not the roof. It just so happened to be eye level with the neighboring roof.

I felt Kay's eyes on me for a moment. When I looked up at her, she gave the man a glance.

"Kind of a perfect angle we've got here, wouldn't you say?" It was a rhetorical question just to let me know she saw it too.

"We're live in thirty," Nick said, securing the camera to its tripod.

"Good to go," she said, turning on her mic and stepping to her mark. Several seconds later, the red light on the camera blinked on, and Kay went to work while I continued to scroll through profiles.

"This is Kathryn McCoy with the *exclusive* aerial shot from atop the Walker Center of what appears to be a suicide attempt in the downtown Salt Lake City area. We are told that the man you are seeing now appeared on the edge of the twelfth-floor ledge of the Hotel Monaco no more than ten minutes ago. So far, authorities have been unsuccessful in their attempts to talk the man down."

The hot September afternoon made it very easy to see the authority of whom Kay spoke. Leaning out of a window, and nearly within touching distance of the man, the officer trying to talk the jumper down looked out of his element and bore no obvious emblems of rank. Just a regular cop. Why wasn't someone trained for this type of situation in his place? It would certainly make my job of flipping through photos go a lot faster if I could see his rank. No matter—I'd find him.

"Hundreds have gathered on the street below," Kay was saying. "There are no words to describe the mood here, but the tension is palpable as we all hope for a peaceful ending to this dramatic situation."

There was a brief silence as Kay listened to the anchors broadcasting from the station, and I could see Kay resisting the urge to press her earpiece into her ear to hear better. She never let herself do that when she thought she was in full frame. It was a pet peeve of hers.

"Don't worry, John, I'm not going anywhere," she said after a few seconds. She then smiled a plastic smile until Nick signaled they were through feeding.

She stooped to retrieve her notepad. "They're cutting to Rich for some statement from the police captain on ground level. We're the only station with an aerial view." She allowed herself a smug smile as I found the officer's profile and raised my binoculars to double check.

"Quick, Rhea, I need facts to highlight," Kay said, clicking her pen and looking at me expectantly.

I listed off some suicide facts while glancing over Officer Dahl's profile. I'd heard that name before. Dahl had been a responding officer several times in the last case I worked, but we'd never met. Too bad, because the guy was a hottie—the kind of guy that had the DNA to make even Kay trip in her heels. If things played out right, I might just have a front row seat to their meeting.

Kay scribbled my facts down in a shorthand only she could read, tossed her pen away, and faced the camera while Nick reframed her.

Magic time.

Anyone who met Kay saw a woman who needed nothing more than her looks to get by in this world. She was a walking Barbie doll, complete with a Hollywood smile, blonde hair, and blue eyes that stopped you mid-step.

But Kay was more than gorgeous. She was brilliant. I never knew which was sharper: her mind or her tongue, but it didn't matter. The woman could talk herself out of any corner and convert any critic. It was her gift to know exactly where to push and for how long to get her way.

"Thank you, Veronica and John," she said with appropriate

solemnity. "As of yet, the police have been unable to identify the man behind me. For those of you watching at home, please take a good look at this man. Someone out there must know who he is and why he may be feeling so desperate as to threaten his own life. Does he have a wife? Children? Most certainly he is somebody's son or neighbor. If you recognize this man, please call the number on the bottom of your screen."

There was silence as she listened to someone speak from the station.

"That's right, John," Kay replied. "The mood downtown is very subdued, and it's heartwarming to see complete strangers pray for this man's well-being. Even now, many stories above the gathering crowds, I can hear the occasional shouted affirmation. This man's got a lot of people cheering for him now, which has to count for something."

Silence, plastic smile, and then, "Well, Veronica, according to statistics, only one in every twenty-five suicide attempts is successful, so we can only hope this will be one of the twenty-four unsuccessful attempts."

More silence.

"You're right, Veronica, we rarely hear about suicides, despite the fact that more Americans, and specifically Utahns, die by suicide than by homicide. It's the third leading cause of death in people ages fifteen to twenty-four, and white males are the demographic at highest risk. Unfortunately, there is a shroud of shame that seems to keep so many of us from talking about this openly, when in many cases, the situation is created by nothing more than the effects of untreated depression. No doubt this is a man well loved by those who know him, but some change in his life apparently has him thinking that he cannot face another day."

While someone at the station spoke, Kay snuck a look down at her paper and gave a solemn nod.

"You're so right, John, but even though jumpers tend to

fall in the TV spotlight, only two percent of all suicides are from falling or jumping."

I beamed with pride, watching her turn all my little tidbits into a flowing story. Not everyone could do that.

Trusting Kay to do her job impeccably as always, I tuned her out and looked back to the jumper. He was now making emphatic motions with his hands, and Dahl was nodding in response.

I glanced over to Kay, who was still talking. That she chose to narrate events meant Kay knew there was no visual tension to hold her viewers. The station was committed to the story now. They couldn't just cut back to *Oprah* or whatever else they might be pre-empting while a man's life hung in the balance. People needed closure when it came to seeing a guy one step from death.

I sighed and again congratulated myself on the brilliant foresight it took to avoid a career in newscasting, even though that's what I had my degree in. In college, Kay and I had always talked about how we would work for competing channels and scoop each other. Kay had lived up to her promise; I had been the one to bail by becoming a private investigator.

Strangely enough, I never heard Kay complain about how things had turned out.

I was glancing down at my watch when a cheer erupted several stories beneath me. I looked to the jumper and smiled. Officer Dahl was reaching over the ledge and offering a hand to the jumper, who was reaching back in return to where Dahl safely stood. Then he disappeared inside the window.

The end.

I sighed in relief that it was a happy ending, because it certainly wasn't the case in all suicide attempts.

"That's right, Veronica," Kay was saying. "It appears the officer has somehow convinced the man to leave the ledge. What the officer said exactly is anyone's guess." Silence. Then,

"Me too, Veronica. Me too."

She smiled her plastic smile a few more seconds, nodded, and held position.

"And . . . end transmission," Nick said.

Kay dropped her anchor-face in a flash and literally pushed her cameraman back toward the door.

"Go! Go! Are we leaving anything?"

"My bag," Nick called out, confused by her frantic flurry of activity. "Where are we going?"

Her face flashed shock at his cluelessness. She walked up to Nick, gripped his chin in her hand, and physically turned his face to the other building.

"Did you see that cop?" she asked like an impatient parent.

"Yes," Nick stammered, obviously shocked by her unusual interpersonal skills.

"That cop just became a hero, and it's our job to introduce him to the world. Now pick up your camera and run!"

Ah, back to old times, I couldn't help but think. Watching Kay like this brought back memories of when we were overachievers at UCLA. I was never as die-hard as Kay was, but I can't say I didn't benefit from her . . . tenacity? Was that a good word for it? Enthusiasm? Dedication? I always tried to think of positive words to explain her passion for newscasting, because heaven knew there were enough people coming up with less favorable ones.

Poor Nick. Once he got used to Kay, he would love her—from a distance. Every cameraman who worked with Kay so far either went somewhere big or quit the business altogether.

Kay barked for me to pick up Nick's bag as she simultaneously pushed Nick in the direction of the door that led off the roof and toward the main building. "You drop that camera and you're through," Kay warned. "You hear me?"

Nick jogged away, muttering some not-so-nice words. Once Kay was sure he wasn't looking back, she let out a smile.

"He's got potential, don't you think?"

I picked up his bag. "You always did like the ones fresh out of school."

She nodded. "Easier to train. Now get a move on. We've got a story to finish."

Trotting after Nick, I couldn't help but ask, "Do you know who that cop is?"

"Not a clue," she said, starting down the ladder ahead of me. I handed the bag down and then made sure the trapdoor was locked behind me when I was far enough down the ladder.

"His name is Officer Dahl. He's former military and a good cop. He covers all the bases and follows protocol."

She jotted the name down, beaming. "I could kiss you for knowing that!"

We started down the stairs, Kay making unusually good speed for someone in her attire.

"He won't give an interview," I added. Kay glared back at me as if that were my fault, even as her shoes clicked down the stairs. "He'll defer to rank," I continued. "He's modest."

"Modest?" Kay snorted. "I've never met a truly modest person in my life. Everyone wants to feel special. *Everyone* likes to be noticed."

I smiled at her conviction. "I'm just telling you that if you or any other reporter walks up to him with a mic, he will disappear."

"Hmph," was her only response, and we were quiet until we reached the twenty-fourth floor. Nick was there, holding the door open for us. I handed him his bag back.

"You guys take the elevator," I said. "I'll use the stairs."

"Why?" Nick asked in pure confusion.

"Because she's paranoid and superstitious," Kay snapped, reminding him once again that cameramen shouldn't try to think. "Now go call the elevator."

Nick nodded and did as he was told. Kay watched him with a hint of satisfaction as he scampered away.

"*You're* the paranoid and superstitious one," I argued playfully. "I'm the sneaky and elusive one."

"Hence the stairs," she agreed. "I need time to fix my makeup in the elevator, so meet me on the corner outside, okay? You can point this Officer Dahl out to me."

I nodded and we ran. Or rather, I ran and Kay primped. All I could think was, *Why did I ever move from California?*

Oh well. It was a moot point, really, seeing as how Kay had followed me to Utah. All's well that ends well, right?

Ten flights later, I exited the stairwell into the bright afternoon sun and, careful not to look at Kay, moved to stand next to her. Both of us kept our eyes on the gathering group of reporters.

"You're right," Kay said. "The guy they're shoving mics at is not the one from the roof. Where is he?"

I felt an odd moment of hesitation, but I got over it pretty quickly.

"There," I said, indicating for her to look straight ahead. "Dark hair and barrel chest. He's the one writing a report."

I looked back at Kay, surprised to see her momentarily stunned.

"Do you see him?"

She slowly nodded. "He's younger than I would have thought."

"And hot?" I offered.

She avoided the teasing tone in my voice and held out her hand to Nick. "Lav mic, now!"

Nick jumped to action, pulling the body mic from his bag.

"Is he married?" Kay asked, her voice all business.

"No. Divorced, no children. He lives just a few miles from here."

Seeing that Nick's face was buried in his bag, she allowed herself another smile. "Man, it's good to have you back."

"L.A. was that dull without me, huh?"

"Completely. And I swear traffic got worse too."

I laughed. "Well then, welcome to Utah, where the natives think that taking forty-five minutes to travel thirty miles in five o'clock traffic is too much to be borne."

Her lips puckered in amusement. "Bless their hearts."

Nick stood, holding the lav mic proudly in his right hand. "Got it!"

She deftly hooked herself up, snapping instructions to Nick as she did so. "I want that camera on extreme zoom, and you have to keep this mic within range while staying completely out of sight. Do you understand?"

Nick nodded, and I contented myself to watch. My job was done. It was time for Kay to work her side of our magic.

"When I go talk to that officer, I want you zoomed in on him so it looks like you're two feet away."

"But there's—"

Kay held up her hand for silence. "Okay?"

Poor Nick sighed in resignation, and I sat on a nearby granite block for my front row seat to watch what was about to unfold across the street. I had an idea of what Kay was up to, but I couldn't believe she was actually going through with it. That's where she and I differed drastically. She could defy every social construct known to man to such a degree that no one knew what she was up to. Too often, men were so struck by her beauty that it took them a while to honestly consider what someone like her saw in someone like him.

By then, it was too late.

"I'm going to have to stand really close," she whispered, mostly to herself. "I hope his voice is as big as he is."

Then she was off.

Picking up Nick's headphones, I asked, "Can I wear these?"

Looking whipped, he nodded.

"Don't worry," I said. "I'll let you know if there are any technical difficulties."

He did nothing more than shrug. Poor kid. Kay had really done a number on him.

"You know," I said off-handedly, "Kay's last camera man makes six figures a year now."

That caught his attention, and I offered him a wink.

"Use her as much as she uses you," I advised. "She won't mind one bit."

That said, I put on the headphones and listened in.

WHILE KAY RACED back to the station with her prize interview, I made my way to the airport to pick up my favorite missionary. Former-Elder Andy Wright came down the escalator with a carry-on, a backpack, and a smile that belonged in Disneyland. The kid was going to break hearts in Provo.

I looked the guy over and had to smile. Back in California, I'd only ever seen him in a suit. He was a missionary at the time, and I was just a random girl on the street with zero desire to talk to him. Since then, I'd pictured him a lot of ways in the "real world," but never as a J. Crew kid. His outfit—and yes, it was an honest-to-goodness coordinated outfit—was a walking ad for preppy *chic*. With new jeans that hadn't been washed yet and a shirt that had yet to form to his body even after a day flying across the country, Andy was like a little kid dressed for his first day of school. Only school didn't start until January for him. He was coming out to Utah early to find a job and get the lay of the land before he started school.

When he approached me, I held out my hand out of habit. "Hey there, Elder."

"It's Andy, actually," he said, releasing his carry-on and throwing his arms around me in a big bear hug.

I laughed and hugged him back. "Andy, then."

When he pulled away, I noticed something was different. Looking him up and down, I tried to figure it out. Then our eyes met again and it hit me. "Did you grow?"

He blushed as I looked down at his shoes and noted the thick soles. Whoops. No, he hadn't grown. He was wearing raisers.

"You look good," I said before things could get awkward.

Bless his soul, the boy actually blushed deeper.

"Can I help you with your bags?" I asked, pointing to the belts behind us. "Which one is your stuff coming out on?"

"I'm shipping it," he said, gripping his carry-on again. "This is all I got."

"All right," I said, gesturing the direction I had parked. "Then your carriage awaits."

He adjusted the bag on his shoulder, watching me as he did so. "You look fantastic, Rhea. Really fantastic."

"Thanks," I said, deciding that looking even halfway decent was halfway to a miracle after cooking on the top of a windy skyscraper. "How was your flight?"

"Good," he said, as we headed up to the parking terrace. "I just can't believe I'm here, you know? I've seen pictures my whole life, but never actually been to Salt Lake. Can we stop by the temple on the way to your house?"

I checked my watch, noting that Kay's broadcast would begin in thirty minutes—her first broadcast in Utah. "How about we get you situated first? We'll walk there after dinner."

Eyes aglow, he nodded and followed me through the automatic doors where the arid, Utah air hit us the moment we walked outside.

"Whoa, it's like an oven here!" Andy said in shock.

"Dry heat," I agreed. "I miss the humidity."

"Yeah," he agreed, but his enthusiasm quickly returned. "Do you like living here?"

A grin tugged at my face, and I kept things simple. "Yeah."

Did I ever, in a million years, think that I would live in Utah? No. Would I have bet the farm that Kay would die before she spent a week in the place? In a heartbeat. But would I be missing out on dating the best guy on the planet had I not moved to Salt Lake? Without a doubt.

Technically, Ty and I had only been dating for four weeks, but if he wasn't the guy for me, then I was destined to be a nun. My whole life, I'd imagined that my best friend, Ben, was the only guy I could put up with. Ty had proved me wrong

With a push of a button, I popped the trunk for Andy's stuff, surprised when he stopped in his tracks.

"Everything okay?" I asked.

He hesitated, staring at my Audi. "That's yours?"

I looked back at my baby and realized Andy was seeing it for the first time—just like I had in the lot—with awe, respect, and outright desire.

The Audi R8 V10 could go zero to sixty in under five seconds and drove like a fantasy come to life. Like everyone else on the planet, I'd seen it in *Iron Man*. Like everyone else, I'd wanted it. But unlike most everyone, I had the connections to actually get one. And I loved it. Deeply.

"Beautiful, isn't it?"

His mouth fell open, momentarily robbed of coherent words. I knew how he felt. While he gawked, I threw his stuff into the trunk.

"Are you serious?" he breathed. "This is what you drive?"

It was hard not to laugh. "No, I rented it to impress you."

He caught my sarcasm, his eyes filling with wonder as he touched it with reverence. "I'm going to need pictures to send to my friends. They'll die when they see this!"

"Sure," I agreed. "We can take them at my place."

"Totally," he agreed, and we set off.

THREE

SNAGGING THE REMOTE as we walked in, I turned on the TV. My DVR was recording the evening news, but I still wanted to see it live.

"Do you need something to drink?" I asked Andy. "Coconut water? Bottled water?"

His nose wrinkled. "Coconut water?"

"Regular water it is," I laughed. "Go ahead and leave your luggage by the door. Ty will be over in a bit to take you to his place."

Andy pushed his carry-on against the wall and dropped his backpack next to it as he looked around the living room and its vintage touches. "This house could be a bed and breakfast."

"Only if I redid the outside to match," I agreed, tossing him a bottled water as the opening credits for the evening news flashed onto the screen. The jumper should be the lead story, so I moved to the couch. A face I knew well filled the screen. Veronica Redgrave, anchorwoman for the evening and nightly news on Kay's new channel, informed viewers in somber tones of the day's dramatic events while Kay appeared in a split screen.

"Hey, I remember her," Andy said, twisting the lid off his water and bobbing his head at Kay on the screen. "She was at your baptism, right?"

"Right," I agreed, watching Kay's carefully practiced "concerned" face wait for its turn to speak. She had returned to her spot on the roof where we had recorded earlier.

". . . reporting live from the scene is our own Kathryn McCoy," Veronica said, her voice matching her somber expression. "What is the feeling downtown after today's events, Kathryn?"

"The attempted suicide was resolved earlier this afternoon, Veronica, and the city's inhabitants seem to be back to business as usual." Kay pointed behind her. "But two hours ago, the man on that ledge, who police have now identified as Salt Lake City resident Mark Epson, had the downtown area at a standstill."

The report cut to B-roll footage recorded earlier and zoomed in on the man in question. Kay's rookie cameraman had done his job well. In the shot, Officer Dahl had yet to establish fluid contact, and the man peered down to the ground below. In the background, Kay's pre-recorded voice narrated what the audience was seeing in this exclusive footage.

"Wow, it's not often you see a jumper," Andy said while sipping his water. It was true, at least for the news. Jumpers usually didn't vie for so much attention—especially if they were serious. That, combined with what a zoom lens was now confirming what I had earlier considered to be a confident posture, had me wondering how legitimate this incident had been. Had it merely been a distraction to divert attention away from something else going on?

That was my background in Hollywood showing through, but the suspicion still had me itching to whip out my laptop and see what else was happening downtown this afternoon. Were any bills passed at the State Capitol? Was there a large stock trade? Were other glamorous stories pre-empting regular programming in other states? It would make me feel better to look all that up, but I had a guest. Following up on my random suspicions would have to wait until Andy was tucked away at Ty's house.

"I'm glad he didn't do it," Andy said just as footsteps came up my front steps. I recognized their cadence easily and didn't need to look up to know Ty was coming through my front door. But I looked anyway, catching his smile as our eyes met.

"Hey, beautiful," he said, crossing to my chair and dropping a kiss on me. Then he politely turned to Andy and offered his hand. "You must be Andy. I'm Ty, Rhea's boyfriend."

There was a slight hesitation as Andy assessed Ty before offering his hand in return. Their hands clasped and pumped stiffly. "Andy Wright."

"Great to have you," Ty said, releasing his grip and moving a step my direction. "I hope you're hungry because dinner's my treat. You like Indian, sushi, or a varied menu?"

"Varied," Andy said, casting a look at me. "But I was planning on paying."

"Nuh-uh," Ty said, heading toward the kitchen. "Rhea doesn't let guests pay, so it's either me or her footing the bill. No arguments." He grabbed a glass from the cabinet and grabbed himself some water from the dispenser in the fridge.

It was a smart move on his part, increasing the distance between him and Andy while Andy pouted about having another guy buy him dinner. Ty was right—my guests didn't buy food when they were staying with me. It was a rigid rule, and I wasn't about to bend it for something as trivial as male pride.

That Ty was modifying the rule so he could pay was something I should have foreseen. Then again, I couldn't love a guy who wasn't a step ahead of me some of the time.

"Something close," I suggested to Ty. "Andy wants to walk around Temple Square after dinner."

"Tin Angel?" Ty offered, and I nodded.

"Perfect."

Glancing back to the screen, I realized I had missed Kay's entire broadcast, but I could watch it later on the DVR. Kay would be here the second she left the station to dissect it and dish on her first day.

"Can't I treat you as a thank you for letting me stay with you for a few days?" Andy asked us.

"Nope," Ty and I said together, earning a frown from Andy. He'd get over it.

* * *

The evening heat went unmentioned as a pair of sister missionaries gave us the official tour of Temple Square. Based on Andy's expression, the visit was equivalent to finding the lost city of Atlantis, and I tried to focus on his enthusiasm as the sister missionaries recited facts I'd already committed to memory. I'm weird like that. I sit on a stakeout for hours at a time and never get impatient, but you start telling me something I already know—especially if it's packaged like something new and exciting—and suddenly my patience goes up in smoke.

"Your foot's tapping," Ty whispered to me as we sat for the acoustical demonstration in the Tabernacle.

I stilled it, but Ty snickered when I stole a glance at my watch a moment later. Kay should be calling soon. Also, this tour was taking forever.

"Can you believe this architecture?" Andy asked from the other side of me. "It's totally unreal the effort people put into things back then."

"Totally," I agreed. Modern man may be impressed with his skyscrapers, but he'd lost touch with building anything by hand. Buildings like the Mormon Tabernacle were a thing of the past.

"I just think of all the pioneers sacrificed to make these buildings," Andy whispered as one of our guides took her place at the pulpit for the demo. "It took generations of families to make it what it is." The few dozen people in the Tabernacle hushed just in time for my phone to vibrate in my pocket.

Knowing it was Kay, I peeked at the text as the demo began: *BREAKING NEWS. Headed to your place. We NEED to talk!*

At least Kay wasn't bored. She'd been on the clock all of eight hours in Utah, and so far things had been hopping.

On a tour at Temple Square, I typed back. *Home in 45.*

"That Kay?" Ty whispered as I sent the message. I nodded as the sister missionary tore a piece of paper, the sound echoing around the room.

"Wow," Andy breathed, mesmerized by the resonance of the hushed sound in the massive room. I smiled at him as my phone vibrated again.

Ditch them and get over here! I need you! This is huge!!!

Ty peeked over my shoulder to read it, and I let him.

"That girl is a trip," he whispered. "You're not going to bail on your elder's dream tour, are you?"

He was right, of course. I needed to stay. But that didn't mean I had to like it.

Thirty's the best I can do, I typed back, earning a raised eyebrow from Ty as the final pin fell to end the demo.

"That's so cool," Andy said, turning to me. "They didn't need microphones back then." His eyes dropped to my phone. "Who was that texting you?"

"Kay," I said, opting for honesty. "She's trying to get me to ditch you and help her with some breaking news."

"I see." His eyes glanced between Ty and me. "Well, if you need to go—"

"I told her thirty minutes," I said as the sister missionaries rejoined us. "We have time to finish."

"Good. Because I'm glad you're here with me." His hand reached out and squeezed mine in an innocent gesture, although Ty's reaction next to me made it seem like more. I squeezed Andy's hand back and released.

"Glad to be here," I said.

"Me too," Ty grumbled so only I could hear.

If Andy felt any of the awkwardness of the next twenty minutes, he gave no sign. On one side of me, I had a guy fulfilling a lifelong dream. On the other side, Ty was watching closely to see how many times I would check my phone for the time. His mocking smirk only made me feel worse about wanting to bail on the tour and meet up with Kay. Poor Andy—he hadn't even been with me four hours, and already I wanted to pawn him off to go work.

Thanks to my father's valiant effort in my upbringing, I resolved to stay with Andy as we exited the gates of Temple Square, but a rather nagging part of me wished he would disappear for a few hours.

"How about this," Ty said as we headed for his truck. He turned to Andy. "What do you say we ditch Rhea and just you and me tour the Conference Center? Trust me, you don't want to be around her and Kathryn when they get down to it."

I could have kissed him, then and there, if it wouldn't have clued Andy in to the sly favor Ty was pulling for me. I tried to keep the hope out of my eyes as I turned to Andy and saw him hesitate.

"It's true," I added. "My dad would never forgive me for leaving you to go work, but the sooner I meet with Kay, the sooner you'll have my full attention."

Andy's expression softened. "How can I argue with that? Get out of here, then. We'll meet up at your place after the other tour."

I was already jogging away.

"Wait!" Andy called after me. "How will you get home?"

"She'll run," Ty answered for me as he headed for the crosswalk. "C'mon, man. More touring joy awaits."

I felt Andy's eyes on me as I started the run home. I turned and shot him one last wave before crossing the street and sprinting to my place, where Kay's car sat in my driveway. I ran up the stairs and found her sitting on the loveseat in my living room. I wasn't surprised to see her replaying my recording of her broadcast. What did surprise me was that she had the footage paused on a clip that didn't have her in it.

"What is it?" I asked. "Because I went against everything my father has ever taught me to get here."

She glanced at the door. "And you ditched the guys?"

"With Ty's help, yes. What's up?"

She reclined against the back of the loveseat. "We, my friend, have an honest to goodness scandal on our hands."

She looked so pleased, I knew it had to be good. "Yeah?"

"See that guy?" she asked, pointing to the jumper on the screen. "Mark Epson, right?"

"That's what police say," I agreed.

"Well, Mark and his wife, Julie, disagree. They claim Mark was sick all day with food poisoning. That man up there is a double."

Now I understood why she had the footage paused on a close-up. She was looking for something to prove the story.

"Add to that the news that the jumper here disappeared from the mental hospital he was checked into before the *real* Mark Epson and his wife reported the doppelganger claim, and the door is open for controversy."

"But the fingerprints were a match for Mark Epson in the system, right?" I asked.

"Please, Rhea, we both know those can be faked."

I nodded, moving up to the screen. "But you can't report on his claim unless you have something to substantiate it. I mean, technically the guy is mental, right?"

"Right," she agreed. "Which is why I need you. This could be huge if we can find anything to hang their story on."

Indeed, in Kay's hands, it could be just the story to kick her from daytime to nighttime news.

"Have you met the Epsons?" I asked.

She held up a DVD. "Of course. I had to get footage for comparison. I need your eagle eye to get to the bottom of this."

All guilt for ditching Andy vanished as I felt my body still and focus.

"Let me grab my laptop," I said, running to my bedroom. To see if the two men were one and the same, I needed to see these images side by side. If necessary, I would pull the footage off my DVR and compare them on the computer, but two different screens and the human eye might just be enough.

"So Ty and Andy are on a man date?" she called from the living room. "They must be thrilled about that."

"They'll be fine," I said, snatching my case and heading back her way.

"Think they'll duel over you before Andy moves down to Provo?"

"It's not like that," I said, walking back into the living room.

"Honey, it's always like that," she drawled.

I ignored the comment and fired up the computer, holding my hand out for the disc.

"I didn't realize it at the time," she said, pointing to the TV, "but this guy is really covered up for how hot it was today. You'll notice that Mark Epson is in shorts and a T-shirt in that video. The guy on this ledge is in slacks and long-sleeve button-up—and not the Mr. Mac stuff everyone wears around here. High end. I'm thinking Canali."

"And the other Mark Epson?" I asked, entering my password.

"No style to speak of. You'll see. But in his defense, he's been puking all day, so he claims, so random rags are appropriate."

I inserted the disc and looked at the TV screen while my viewer loaded. Kay was right. It hadn't seemed significant at the time, but the man was overdressed for an afternoon that was close to hitting a hundred degrees. But, "Gee, he's totally overdressed to be out on that ledge. He must be hot," isn't one of your first thoughts when someone is a hundred feet off the ground and threatening to drop. Both the shirt and slacks were definitely Canali. I should have noticed, since the designer was all but unknown in Utah from what I had seen.

I was going to have to broaden my focus while working in Utah. In L.A., a detail like that wouldn't matter. In Salt Lake, it absolutely did.

Kay's footage of the other Mark Epson had been taken in the lobby of the police station. She must have camped there based on a lead. The police station reminded me about her interaction with one Officer Ken Dahl.

I seriously wasn't going to get over that name for a while.

"So, did you go to the station to get this footage specifically, or did you just happen to be hanging around waiting for a certain cop to get off duty?"

"Shut up," she said quickly.

"What? He's your type."

"Anatomically," she agreed, her voice heavy with annoyance. "Which, of course, means he's deeply flawed in other ways."

"Such as?"

"Such as being a Mormon," she snapped. "Let's compare hairlines first."

Ah, one of the few insurmountable obstacles for Kay. Given the choice between a Mormon boy and a convicted felon, her family would probably opt for the latter. Not that Kay even pretended to care what her family thought, but still. Her dating an active Mormon was a bad, bad idea. Yet it seemed tragic somehow that the perfect Ken Dahl should be kept from Reporter

Barbie over something as simple as religion.

"I should have grabbed the mug shot," she muttered. "That would give us a better shot of his hairline."

"On it," I said, jumping online and quickly finding desired image. For the sake of convenience, I made it the wallpaper on my computer and brought the video back up.

Familiar with each other's methods, we were both quiet for a few moments as we looked things over.

"Different guys?" she said after a few minutes.

"Different guys," I agreed.

"The jaw," she said, outlining it with her finger.

"Too square on the jumper," I agreed. "And look at the tan line on the jumper's pointer finger. He usually wears a ring there. The other Mark doesn't have that."

"Good catch," she cooed. "I wasn't looking at his hands. He's kind of hot."

"And married," I added.

"Huh," was her only response.

She looked back and forth between the laptop and the TV several more times. "The hair's close, but off; the clothes are completely wrong; and I would guess that the real Mark Epson weighs about twenty pounds more than the jumper. Maybe that was another reason for all the clothes." Letting out a puff of air, she leaned back to think. "But why? Why would one guy go to this length to frame another guy for attempted suicide? It's totally bizarre. Rob a bank or something. That, at least, makes sense."

"Maybe you need to get to know Mark Epson better. I'll bet you that something in his history will tell us why we're dealing with an exhibitionist rather than a bank robber."

"No bet," Kay said, dialing her phone to call her new producer. The woman was going to weasel herself into a night broadcast after her first day on the job. They say success is 90 percent luck and 10 percent timing. Kay possessed both qualities in spades and had enough left over to charm a small country.

While she pitched the angle to the producer, I let the DVR play again and watched the doppelganger with fresh eyes. He'd pulled off an elaborate ruse and must have known that it would fall apart under scrutiny. So why do it at all?

I watched his eyes. Cold, steady, and precise. My guess was that he was former military, which was something else I should have picked up on. My phone buzzed in my pocket, but I ignored it, watching the TV and listening to Kay wrangle her producer into a meeting with the night producer on duty. Just as her conversation was coming to a close, I heard two sets of feet move up my front steps.

Ty and Andy were back so soon?

I grabbed my phone out of my pocket just in time to read the new text before they came in the door. *No tour guides on duty at the Conference Center. Be at your place in a sec.*

A "sec" was right. Ty and Andy came in the front door just as Kay exited the kitchen.

"Kathryn!" Ty said, opening his arms for a hug. Kay walked right into them.

"Hate to hug and run, but my paycheck calls."

"By all means, ditch me then," Ty said, giving her one last squeeze.

Stepping away from Ty, Kay gave Andy a quick once over and sent me a snide look. I knew what she was thinking. It was the same thing I'd thought when I first saw him in the airport.

"Nice outfit," she said with a level of loathing only females would pick up on. Poor Andy blushed with pleasure.

"Thanks. I got it just before coming out here."

"Never would have guessed," she said, ejecting the DVD from my computer and putting it back in its case. She glanced at Ty. "We'll have to dish dirt another time."

Ty nodded and the two shared one of their covert looks.

Sometimes it felt like they had been plotting siblings in a previous life.

"Well, it was good to see you again," Andy said, inserting himself between Kay and Ty in a way that seemed a little too forced and eager. Ty settled on sending Andy a confused look while Kay had a more direct response, grabbing her purse before squaring off with him.

"Let's be straight, Andy. We are not friends, and it's never good to see you again. You totally screwed over my five-year plan by playing missionary with my friend here."

Andy's chin went up. "You want me to apologize for that?"

Kay headed to the door. "Oh, I wish you could. But I'll settle on you moving to Provo and starting a forever family with some cute co-ed." She opened the door and sent me and Ty a parting wave. "Tootles."

The door shut as Ty and I shared an awkward look.

"Why are you friends with her?" Andy grumbled.

He wasn't looking for a real answer, but Ty gave him one anyway. "Well, there's one thing to be said for Kathryn—you always know where you stand with her."

I smiled and changed the subject. "Anyone want to make dessert?"

FOUR

AFTER I WALKED the boys over to Ty's place, Ty walked me back home. Bless Andy's heart, but he didn't seem to get the hint that Ty and I wanted to be alone for a bit.

"Poor guy hasn't acclimated yet," Ty said as he draped his arm around me and matched our steps. I leaned in, smelling his new cologne and feeling myself melt a little. Diesel. On Ty it smelled fantastic.

"Acclimated to what?" I asked, my mind already forgetting what I was asking and why.

"Being home." Oh yeah. Andy. "People are weird for a while after they get back from their missions. Some switch right over to being back, but others can take a few months. Others are forever weird."

"Which were you?" I asked, reaching my arm around him.

He gave a casual shrug. "My dad died while I was gone, so I was pretty weird when I got back."

Wow. I'd walked him right into that one. It was the cologne's fault. I was tired and distracted, but Ty continued before I could respond.

"But your elder is fighting the change." A wry smile curved one side of his mouth. "Provo will be perfect for him."

"The 'change?' " I laughed, hating how close our houses were to each other and that my walk home was already over. "You make him sound like a vampire."

He glanced at my house. "Well, we're here."

"Yeah." I didn't want him to go, but he would. Even if I asked him in for a bit. "See you in six hours?"

"Oh yeah," he agreed. "Eight or ten miles tomorrow?"

My first thought was for ten, but then I thought of Andy. I needed to be around in case he woke up early. His body was probably still on Eastern time. "Let's go with eight."

"So you can spend more time with the guy who's trying to replace me?" he said, pulling me around to face him. His arms automatically circled my waist.

"Please!" I laughed. "He's not about that. And I think we've made it pretty clear that I'm with you."

Ty shook his head. "He's going to hit on you," he said, his voice sing-songy. "I can feel it in the air."

"Is that your male intuition alerting you?"

"Something like that," he agreed as his eyes fell to my mouth. I could say whatever I wanted at this point—he wasn't listening. He was going to kiss me whether my lips were moving or not. We both leaned in at the same time.

This was why we had wanted a few minutes away from Andy. Connection. It's just not the same with an audience. I'd kissed my fair share of guys—I'd even fancied myself in love with one of them, but the gentle ache that filled my chest when I kissed Ty was a new thing for me. When I pushed in, the pain turned sweet. In order to pull away, I had to tense my body to the point where I momentarily forgot how to breathe.

That's why it was always Ty who pulled away first.

Dating a guy who was always the first to put on the brakes was odd. Even Chad, the model of Mormonhood who I had dated when I first arrived in Utah, hadn't been as contained as Ty. But since Ty was trying to get off the Mormon "naughty" list by meeting with our bishop twice a week, our interactions had to be kept to things he didn't mind sharing with clergy.

But for five too-brief seconds, Ty pulled me in flush against him. His mouth wasn't shy, nor was it forceful. I knew myself well enough to know that it was my trust in him that made his touch so potent. When all ulterior motives are gone and you give in to the moment, something magical happens.

Or maybe Ty was just a good kisser. It was one or the other.

Either way, the moment after I gripped him back and angled in, he stepped away.

"*Hasta mañana*," he said, walking backwards. At least he had the decency to look like he didn't want to go.

"Yeah," I agreed, suddenly thinking that six hours was entirely too much time to sleep. "Be nice to my elder."

He raised his arm, showing me three extended fingers. "Scout's honor." Then he was headed back home.

FIVE

AT 5:05 THE next morning, I stretched my quads outside Ty's front door and wondered if I needed to knock. Being late was so unlike him—although technically he wasn't late yet. He still had twenty more seconds.

When he stepped out the front door, Ty was wearing the work pack he brought when we did ten-mile routes in the morning. He was a personal trainer, and to get to work on time, he had to run straight to the gym and shower.

"I thought we were only doing—" I stopped when Ty gave me a quick shake of his head.

"Morning," he said, giving me a kiss.

"Morning," I replied, more confused than annoyed at having been interrupted. Just then, Andy came out of the front door wearing a pair of Nike shorts and matching shirt. Another outfit. He looked good—like a department store sale ad in the Sunday paper. It was hard not to want to stage a fashion intervention. "You joining us, Andy?"

"Yeah," he said, taking a deep breath of the pre-dawn air. "I miss running. I couldn't do it on the mish."

I smiled to counteract the wave of annoyance radiating from Ty. Running was his sacred time. The only reason he ran with me was because we pushed each other. We were too

29

competitive not to. If Andy was slow, there was no way Ty would wait up for him. Besides, if we slowed up, Ty would be late for work.

"You got eight miles in you?" I asked.

"I guess we'll see!" Andy said, jogging down the steps.

Wrong answer.

Pretending the silence while we stretched was normal, I mentally rerouted our run to a nearby park so Ty could enjoy a decent run and get to the gym in time for his first appointment.

"Down to 300 West for laps at Liberty?" I suggested as we started down the street. I watched the tension between Ty's shoulders relax.

"Sounds good," he agreed.

Andy didn't know north from west in Utah yet, so he trotted along without caring which way we went. "It's so clean here," he commented as we left the Avenues and moved into the downtown area. Streetlights still led our way as the beginnings of dawn peeked over the mountains to the east. A few ambitious birds chirped in nearby trees, and the dew from the night made the air moist and clean, just like Andy said. In six hours, though, this same air would be as hot and dry as an oven.

"Yeah," I agreed and started explaining our route to him, but he interrupted before I could finish.

"Don't worry. I'm pretty sure I can keep up with a girl. Just lead the way."

He was kidding. Kind of. But even though I was fine blowing the comment off, it didn't mean that I didn't secretly enjoy the flash of annoyance in Ty's eyes.

"Good," Ty said, picking up the pace. "You won't mind if we up to our usual speed, then."

Andy had just been called out, which should be interesting. Ty didn't mind people talking big, as long as they delivered.

Our usual pace was for five-minute miles, but this felt a little faster. I didn't have to guess why. As Ty and I fell in step next to each other, Andy's footfalls became heavier in our wake.

"You're being mean," I whispered.

"I told him I wouldn't slow down for him before he left the house," he said, looking straight ahead. "But he was all giddy to see you again."

I managed a short laugh. "I told you it wasn't like that, Ty."

"Maybe not for you," he muttered, timing his phrases with exhales. "But that guy's got an idea of you in his head, and trust me—he's in love with it."

I really didn't want to hear this. Andy was my missionary. Without him, I wouldn't even know Ty, and there was definitely no chance I'd be a Mormon living in Utah.

"Just leave it alone, okay?"

For a moment he didn't answer. "As long as he keeps a lid on it, I will too."

"Thanks," I said, tuning back into the slapping footfalls behind us. "Now, can we slow down a bit before he collapses?"

We made good time to the park, and Andy stayed close the entire way. Once we got there, though, he slowed to a walk and waved us on.

"I'll find you when we head back," I called to him, and he nodded.

Ty made no comment as we ran along, but his expression spoke volumes.

"I usually don't like jealous guys," I said, "but I'll admit, you wear it well."

He grunted. "Glad to entertain you."

I tried to run along in silence, but it was hard to get into a rhythm when your running partner was involved in some sort of pout fest.

"What happened last night?"

He shook his head, but five seconds later he gave in to the urge to vent. "I know he's your missionary, or whatever, but Rhea, the guy is . . . uppity."

I fought a smile at his word choice and lost. "Oh. Are you not good enough for me, Ty?"

To my dismay, he didn't smile. "I'm trying, okay? I'm trying hard, but I've got baggage!"

"Whoa," I said, touching his arm and slowing us to a stop. "Ty, you can't start thinking like that, okay? If we start stacking up and comparing sins, I'm the one who's going to sink with that ship, got it?"

"But I've—"

"Had some fun with alcohol and pretty ladies?" I asked, keeping my expression unimpressed. "I'm over it. And I'm pretty sure God is too. You're the only one who needs to let go here."

It was clear he didn't believe me. "I try. . . ." Whatever the end of that sentence was, he didn't finish it, so I did it for him—by pushing up on my toes and giving him a kiss.

"You *succeed*, Ty," I said softly. "Now we're thirty seconds behind pace, so get your butt moving."

I took off, knowing he would catch up with me in no time.

ANDY AND I made our way back to my place at a pace that barely passed for a jog. The poor guy was going to be sore but wouldn't slow to a walk when I offered.

"No, this is good. I don't want to slow you down," was his reply.

If Ty had been there, Andy would have been left in the dust the moment those words were uttered. Maybe introducing those two so soon hadn't been my best idea. But Ty had offered to let Andy stay with him. Of course, I knew Ty had ulterior motives; still, I figured once he met Andy, everything would smooth over.

But Ty was right. Something was different with Andy. I didn't want it to be, but it was there. Should I address it? Could I just leave it and let it dissolve organically?

When in doubt, ignore it. It was something my aunt said all the time that made my dad cringe. In this situation, however, I thought she just might be right. I was so lost in thought that I was two blocks away from my house before I looked up from my own shoelaces and slowed my pace. I wasn't aware I had stuck my hand out to slow Andy until the flat of my hand pressed against his chest. His abrupt flinch from my touch was so dramatic, I would have laughed under different circumstances. As it was, the black SUV parked under my tree had me on full alert.

Sure, there was nothing illegal about parking in front of my house, but the Escalade was out of place. Utah had its fair share of black Escalades, but not many cars in Utah gleamed as if they had just been driven off the lot. Nor did they have Nevada plates—Clark County, to be exact—with windows tinted dark enough to have any bored cop issuing a ticket.

And it was parked in front of my house.

"What's wrong?" Andy asked, his eyes following mine to the SUV. "You know them?"

I evaded a direct response. "Work people. Can you do me a favor and split with me right now? Just go right at this next street, then take the next two lefts. It will take you straight to Ty's."

"You don't want them to see me?" he asked, his expression somewhere between hurt and confused. "Seems like I should walk you to your door."

Bad idea. I knew it the moment he said it out loud. No good thing would come of him accompanying me to my front door.

"I just don't like mixing my business life and my personal life," I said, invoking Bambi eyes in hopes he'd be more agreeable. "If you're with me, they'll just stick around longer asking questions. I'd rather just have them go away so we can hang."

That sounded good, right? Like what Ty had said that worked the night before.

"Oh," Andy said, eyeing the SUV as if he too sensed its wonky vibes. "Sure, then. I'll go shower. I'll come over when I'm done."

"Thanks," I said, keeping my face casual as he turned right. I crossed the street to head up the last half block to my house. The men weren't in sight yet, although experience told me there would be two of them. In suits. Expensive suits. The Escalade they drove was light-years away from being the stock model, starting with its TIS10 26-inch rims and Kumho low-profile tires. From a block away, I could tell the grille was STRUT, which meant the interior was tricked out as well. In short, I had a car waiting for me that gangs would kill for. In L.A., that wouldn't be so notable, but in Utah? One might say such an Escalade was as conspicuous as a Canali suit.

Coincidence? Probably not.

My pace slowed as I spotted the two men on my front porch. Judging by their posture, they had been waiting a while, but more alarming than that was their attitude as they did so.

It had been a long time since I had seen "muscle," and I'd never seen it perched on my front steps. Nevermind that neither of the guys looked like stereotypical bouncers at a club. Quite the opposite, in fact. Both men were of average height and weight, with totally normal looks. I couldn't see the bulge of a sidearm under their designer coats, but I knew they were packing—not that they needed bullets. Their stances alone were enough to let even the casual bystander know that they liked to use their conditioned bodies when it came time for action.

Let them do all the talking, I coached myself, crossing my front lawn. I smiled in greeting to each man in turn.

The man nearest to the door stepped forward, identifying himself as the spokesman, while the other man's eyes scanned the street with trained focus. Five-foot-ten with military-cropped brown hair and hazel eyes hidden behind some Clark Kent glasses he didn't need, the spokesman's detached eyes met mine. Oh yeah, he'd killed before and would do it again on command. It seemed like an important thing to take note of. His angular jaw matched his square body, and a gold ring with a black X engraved into it flashed on his left index finger. My old boss had a ring just like it. Again, not likely a coincidence.

"May I help you, sir?" I asked as I approached.

"Elliott sent us," the spokesman said, as if that should mean a whole lot more than it did. Elliott Church was the man I had worked with back in Los Angeles—the only other man I'd seen wearing that ring. For a 15 percent cut, Elliott went out to all the A-list and Who's Who parties, drumming up business for me and other PIs. He met with the clients, settled the bills, and set the astronomical fees. It had been a very profitable arrangement, which had technically ended when I moved to Utah.

Besides, I knew Elliott, and he would warn me before sending these guys my way. One of our cardinal working rules was that I got to choose whether or not to meet the client. And never would he give them my home address. Ever.

Looking into the spokesman's cold eyes, I decided to deal straight with him.

"If Elliott sent you here, he made a big mistake. I'm sure you can understand that I don't like potential clients showing up at my house unannounced at seven in the morning."

"He said you'd be up," he said simply.

His gaze willed me to cower, and I wondered if it might be wise, tactically, for me to do so. It might be best if a man like him underestimated me. I didn't look away, though. Instead, I raised the stakes. "I'm sorry, but I didn't catch your name."

"Sam," he said, purposefully not offering his hand for me to shake. "Sam Collins."

It was a lie, and I let him think I believed it. "Good to meet you, Sam. How can I help you?"

"Would you like to step inside?" he said, motioning to my front door.

"No offense, Mr. Collins, but I don't know you, so if you don't mind, I'd rather stay outside and hear what you have to say."

He reached into his pocket and pulled out a thick envelope, handing it to me. "This is a retainer."

I didn't reach for it. "For?"

His eyes narrowed on me. "Dropping a battle you're going to lose. Elliott likes you, so we're giving you a head's up. Leave the Epson case alone."

Whoa. Not what I was expecting. "And if I don't take this money?" I asked.

He didn't blink. "Someone you know might get hurt."

Hurt. Somehow I didn't think he meant the word the way most people did. "And if I stay out?"

"Everyone will be happy in a week or so." He slapped the envelope into my chest, walking past me and back toward the Escalade. Not sparing me a glance, his companion did the same.

I honestly didn't mean to pick "Sam's" pocket. It was a monumentally stupid thing to do, and yet it was just a reflex to slide the wallet out of his back pocket and into my waistband. This guy was trying to pay me off Mafia-style, and I was swiping his wallet for a peek? I didn't know if this was evidence of me being gutsy or flat-out reckless. I looked at the reinforced fender and bumper of the Escalade and decided it was the latter. This was the wrong time for me to play my usual games.

For one petrified moment, I worried "Sam" might have detected the lift, but he made no indication that he noticed what I'd done, which was all I could wish for. With both men walking away from me, I opened the wallet and flipped through it. According to the legitimate-looking ID, the guy's name was Oliver Westman, and he lived in Vegas. His wallet contained no cash and three credit cards, including a black American Express.

When the muscle of an organization has a Black Card, it kind of gives you a feel of who you're dealing with real fast.

Oliver/Sam stopped and turned. "You done looking at that?" he asked in a calm voice.

He knew. Man, I was out of practice!

"Habit," I said, as if that explained everything, and tossed him the wallet. He caught it without breaking eye contact with me.

"That was a mistake, Ms. Jensen."

"Noted," I agreed.

"Elliott's protection only takes you so far," he warned, and five seconds later he and his friend were in the SUV and on their way down the hill toward downtown.

And I was screwed.

SEVEN

SO I WAS being watched. That was fairly obvious, as was the fact that the technology being used for my surveillance was a step above my pay grade . . . and that was saying something.

The envelope contained fifty thousand dollars, which was my minimum retainer. That they had stuck with paying me my minimum showed a lack of respect on their part. It was a token payment for me to stay out of their way. If I took it, great. If I didn't? Well, Oliver had described that situation perfectly as well: Elliott's protection only took me so far and did not extend at all to people I knew.

Protection? What was my old boss involved with? Granted, I knew the man wasn't completely on the up and up. My first hint had been that he trained me how to do things on the shady side. The second clue lay in the massive paychecks he was always able to draw. I got good gigs when I worked with him. *Really* good gigs.

Had I accepted hush money before? Sure. It just felt different then. In those situations, I had already been on a case, under contract to protect the client's interests. It was part of my contract to not let certain information come to light unless it was subpoenaed.

But this? Someone just walking up to me and saying, *Hey,*

we just framed an innocent guy. Don't look into it, was a little rougher. Adding money into the equation just made it even more corrupt. Instead of the situation being, *Leave it alone or die,* it was, *Leave it alone. Here's some money to remind you that you have no backbone or integrity.*

I cursed under my breath and sank down on my couch to think. The thing I most wanted to do was, of course, on the top of the list of things I shouldn't do: call Elliott. He couldn't tell me anything more than I already knew, and it would just put us both in a more awkward situation. I couldn't talk to anyone about this on the phone at all. Oliver hadn't said so, but talking about it in general was pretty much off limits.

By the time footsteps hopped up my front steps, I had completely forgotten who they belonged to until the door opened and Andy's Disney smile filled the room.

"You got rid of them fast," he said, smelling like Ty's body wash. For some reason that bothered me.

Then it registered that Andy had referred to "them." That meant he had come close enough to look. Not good. I fought for an upbeat smile. "Yeah. They're gone." And currently listening in on this conversation.

He walked over and plopped down on the adjacent loveseat. "I noticed some car dealerships yesterday and thought it might be a good idea to check out some rides today."

"Of course," I said, sitting up and making sure the envelope stayed out of sight. "Let me shower first." It wasn't even 7:30 yet. No dealerships would be open for a bit anyway, and acting normal was crucial—regardless of how unnatural it was.

"Help yourself to anything in the kitchen," I said, heading back to my room. I couldn't help but think that Andy had chosen the worst week possible to come to town. What were the chances of all this happening the week he shows up?

This whole situation was new territory for me, and I needed privacy to process it. Giving the money back was out of the question, but I couldn't keep it either. It was just too twisted. Maybe I could donate the money to some cause where it would do some good. Then I could at least pretend I felt better about turning a blind eye.

Poor Mark Epson. The guy was going to go to a mental hospital. He'd either serve time or pay a massive fine. Not only that, his wife was eight months pregnant. What was so special about Mark Epson that the big bad men of the world wanted to take him out? Dare I hope that he wasn't as innocent as he looked?

I took my time in the shower, trying to convince myself that none of this was really my business. I should just leave things alone and let them unfold. The payoff didn't include forcing Kay to back off. The whole situation would probably resolve itself with or without my involvement. It certainly wasn't worth dying over. And that's what Oliver had been threatening.

I had to let it go. Messing with men like him never ended well.

That decided, I got dressed and took Andy out to search for his dream car.

EIGHT

MY FIRST HURTLE was getting Kay to fly solo on the story. I had to toss our usual pattern of tag-teaming on a story out the window without explanation. For this to come across as natural, I had to wait for her to make first contact. Andy was drooling over a Mini Cooper when I got her first text.

You were right about the tan line on the finger, she wrote. *Not a match for Mark.*

Someone was probably going to get in trouble for that, seeing as how I was certain I wasn't the only one reading her text. To go to such lengths to impersonate someone, just to overlook something so simple had to be infuriating.

Congrats! I texted back. Kay would want something more gushy, but I didn't know what else I could safely say.

On the lot, Andy had settled on cooing over the blue model, and the salesman moved in for the close. I just hoped Andy didn't ask me what I thought of the car. I couldn't find a nice way to say that a guy who purposefully wore raisers shouldn't drive a miniature car. If he wanted to adopt the *Italian Job* persona, he needed an old-school Mini, not a trendy new one. But all in all, he'd probably do better with something reliable, like a Honda.

The real horror of the situation was that Andy's Hollister

outfit kind of matched the car, making the two look like they were made for each other.

I *really* hoped he didn't ask what I thought about the car.

My phone buzzed with a new text from Kay. *Meet me for lunch today?*

I couldn't. And I couldn't tell her why I couldn't. *I'm car shopping with Andy all day,* I texted back. Vague evasiveness. She'd see through it, but I was hoping she'd call me out in person and not via text.

All day?

Think of it this way, I replied. *Once Andy gets a car, he can move to Provo and get a job.* That should get her off my back.

I need your help with this story!!! she texted back before I could tuck my phone in my pocket.

You've got what you need. I know you can take it from here. Have fun! I shoved my phone in my back pocket, promising myself I wouldn't look at it again until I talked Andy into buying car that Ty's truck couldn't run over like a toy.

Or not. It was up to Andy, and it wasn't like I'd be riding in it. Why not let him get what he wanted and drive around in it wearing outfits from ad catalogs with golf clubs hanging out the back? I didn't know for sure if he golfed, but he seemed like the type. And who was I to keep him from expressing himself?

Watching his expression of utter joy as he gripped the steering wheel with reverence, I analyzed my own motives. I saw people with poor fashion sense every day—*all* day, every day, as a matter of fact. I'd thought I'd come to peace with that aspect of living in Utah, and yet with Andy it was different. I didn't want Kay to see him, and I didn't want him to open his mouth around Ty.

What was wrong with me?

"Do you love it?" Andy called to me, hanging his head out the window. I forced a smile.

"Clearly you do!" That was the best I had in me, but I knew it was enough when he beamed. He really was adorable. There was no reason for me to shudder at the thought of him interacting with my friends.

He got out of the car and walked over to me. "I just can't see a down side to it," he gushed, eyes all a-twinkle. I looked at the car, wondering what he saw that I was missing and just stuck with practical critiques.

"Well, you're in snow country and this is a car that floats. Chances of an accident are higher in winter time."

"Please," he scoffed. "I'm from Boston. I know storms."

I wasn't going to argue with him. I'd said my piece. "Well, it sounds like you've made up your mind." My phone buzzed with a text message in my pocket.

"My dad said to keep it under thirty grand."

I had to bite my lip again. Sure, my dad was loaded too, but he'd never bought me a car. If he had, I never would have learned what a car is worth. The same part of me that wanted Andy to dress a little savvier wanted him not to be a guy in his twenties accepting thirty-thousand dollar gifts from Mommy and Daddy—and that's when it hit me.

When I met Andy in L.A., I'd respected him. A lot. And I wanted to keep respecting him. But seeing Andy day-to-day, sans missionary name tag, painted a different picture of the guy I knew a few months ago. Andy was immature. Elder Wright, who I'd listened to and ultimately trusted to lead me in making a monumental change in my life, was now Andy: a spoiled, trendy, twenty-one-year-old guy.

I knew if I thought about this too long, I might just drive myself a little nuts, so I relied on my fallback logic: Without Andy, I never would have met Ty. Without Ty, I would still be hopelessly in love with Ben, who'd gone off and gotten another girl pregnant. And if I had still been in love with Ben, he would have talked me into reducing the mother of his child to a life of single-motherhood while he started a life with me.

I didn't want that to be the truth, but it was.

But because of Andy, Ben was an active father, and I was in love with a guy who somehow seemed to be born with the innate gift of seeing through my crap and still loved me for me. I didn't deserve Ty, but as long as he was on the market, I'd take him. And if some other girl wanted to fight me for rights along the way, well then, bring it on.

Not that Ty made me fight. He was a rather willing captive, as was I. Growing up, I wasn't romantic. I never used to dream of my wedding day, or anything. But if I didn't end up marrying Ty, I had a feeling I might end up a bitter, bitter person.

And that alone was enough to think the world of Andy in his preppy outfits, high-soled shoes, and Daddy-bought car. That was what I needed to focus on.

Stepping away from my side, he walked up and touched the hood. "I think it's perfect," he said at last. "It gets thirty-seven miles per gallon on the freeway, so really, it's cost efficient."

"Take it for a drive then and see if you bond," I suggested. Behind Andy, the salesman grinned, knowing he'd just made a sale. While he grabbed the keys, I checked my most recent text from Kay and chose not to reply.

NINE

WHEN WE GOT back to my place, Kay's hybrid was parked in my driveway. Not good. The noon broadcast was over, so technically she could have been on her lunch, but Kay didn't take a lunch. She was on my front porch because I was ignoring her. There was one thing Kay wasn't, and that's passive. If you piss her off, she gets in your face about it.

Andy was in my car since he had to talk to his parents before buying the Mini, but I suddenly wished I had thought to drop him off at Ty's.

"Hey, it's Kay," Andy said.

"Kathryn," I corrected quickly, giving him a stern look so he would know I was serious. "Don't ever call her Kay, Andy. Got it?"

I could have sworn he rolled his eyes at me but chose to ignore it if he did.

"I hate to ask you to make yourself scarce twice in one day, but do you mind if I talk to Kathryn alone?"

His face crinkled in confusion as he smiled and looked over to Kay. "Seriously? Again?"

"She has to get back to work," I explained. "It'll be fast."

His hand reached for the handle but then paused. "Are you always this secretive, or is it me?"

Uh, both? But really, I'd want to protect anyone I liked from Hurricane Kay.

"You'll just be uncomfortable if you stick around for the conversation," I offered. "I'm trying to save you some awkwardness."

"If you say so," he muttered and opened the door. Kay had already marched down the steps and was halfway to the car.

"Hi, Kathryn," Andy said. I cringed.

"Don't even start," she snapped back. "Just get out of here. I need to talk to that friend of yours."

Andy was momentarily shocked silent before he shot back. "Why do you hate me? What did I ever do to you?"

Kay took the time to send him a proper glare. "You cannot be serious when you ask that unless you are a complete idiot," she said, sliding into the seat Andy had just vacated. "Drive. We need to talk."

I sent Andy a little wave. "I'll be back." He was too stunned to reply as I put my car in reverse and took Kay away from the poor guy.

"Maybe try not to be so rough on the kid," I said before she could launch into her tirade.

"Really? You think I care one inch about his feelings after moving my career from L.A. to Salt Lake City only to have you stonewall me? If I wanted to commit career suicide, I could have chosen much more glamorous ways than moving to Utah!"

I kept my voice calm. "I'm not stonewalling you. Things just got a little complicated."

"Complicated?" she scoffed. "Please explain."

What could I say? How much could I say? The truth was always best. "I had some visitors this morning encouraging me to let you fly solo on this story."

The truth was so bizarre that it took a moment for Kay to process my undertones. "Visitors?" she repeated after several seconds.

I nodded. "Out of state."

Her eyebrows raised. "And they specifically asked you to stay out?"

"Yes."

Intrigue replaced fury as I drove us up to the top of the Avenues and headed down the Gravity Hill loop. After several seconds, she looked at me and then sent pointed looks around the car, asking the silent question, *Is the car bugged?*

I nodded.

Her jaw dropped but not in dismay. The idea actually excited her.

"But *I'm* good, right?" she asked. "I can do my job?"

"Unless they pay you a visit. Then it's up to you," I said, sending a clear message to whoever was listening. They'd said nothing about Kay when they talked to me, so I considered her in the clear.

Kay considered the situation, not looking around at the scenery as I took the turn at the bottom of the loop. "It's kind of offensive that they don't think I can do my job without you—whoever they are. Do they honestly think that by taking you out the equation I won't expose their little ruse?"

I didn't answer, because I didn't know what they wanted. My thumb tapped on my steering wheel as I considered the angles until I was pulled from thought by Kay's chuckle.

"You actually look nervous," she teased. "I don't see that expression on your face very often."

"And you think it's a good thing?"

"Oh, not at all," she said, throwing her hands up. "It pretty much freaks me out, so I've got to laugh about it. And all this going down while you're babysitting your little missionary? Too perfect!"

"I'm not babysitting," I said as the Capitol building came into view. "But the timing does suck."

"Doesn't it always," she agreed, taking a deep breath. "Girl,

I was ready to ream you something fierce. I was worried about that, so thanks for saving me the effort."

"Sure."

Silence.

"I still hate that elder of yours."

"I know."

Another pause. "Sorry he's so easy to be mean to."

"Ty manages to be nice," I shot back.

The jab rolled off her like a bead of water. "Yeah? Well, technically Ty is a saint, so I don't feel bad about not living up to his impossible standards."

I fought to hide a smile as I pointed us back to my house. "Try to be nice?"

She bit her lip, mulling over my request. "He looks at me like he's better than me. He wouldn't say two words to me if it weren't for you, and the only reason he wants to get along with me is so he can look good for you."

That wasn't an agreement to play nice on her side. It was her reason for staying mean.

"Sorry, hon," she sighed, "but I won't do a blessed thing to help that little suck-up look good around you."

When it served her purposes, Kay could role-play with the best of them. She could easily fake it to Andy, but it wasn't fair to force her to.

"I'll try to keep you two apart then," I said. "Can you at least be helpful with that until he's gone? It's only one more night. He'll have his new car tomorrow."

"Can't wait," she huffed as I turned up my street. At the sight of her car, Kay refocused. "I'm going to bust this story open with or without your help. I don't understand why anyone would buy you off to stay out."

I wasn't going to speculate on that anytime soon.

"You hear that, whoever's listening?" she said loudly for any possible microphone. "I'm going to throw this story wide open without Rhea's help—and you can't buy me off!"

Brave words uttered by someone who had no idea who she was talking to. Still, she made me feel totally spineless as I pulled up to my house where Andy sat waiting for me on the front porch swing.

"Try not to talk to him," I suggested.

"No problem," she agreed as we got out of the car. And in a beautiful moment of sense, Andy chose not to speak to Kay either.

TEN

ANDY LOOKED PENSIVE as we walked into my house. Kay and Ty probably would have called his expression judgmental, but I was willing to give Andy the benefit of the doubt. He flopped on my couch, sending me a guarded look as he spun his CTR ring around his right ring finger.

"Your landscaping out front is amazing," he said, although that clearly wasn't what was on his mind.

"Thank you," I said. "Ty and I have put a lot of hard work into it."

"It shows," he said with a nod. "My mom would love your flowers. You have quite the green thumb."

"I get it from my dad," I said, pleased, even though I knew this was only small talk.

He looked at the door, envisioning something that wasn't there. "Kay—"

"Kathryn," I corrected.

Andy shrugged it off. "She's not here."

"Doesn't matter," I pressed. "Just get into the habit."

"Why?" he snapped. "Clearly she hates me no matter what I call her, so I might as well earn her dirty looks."

I shook my head. "Not like that. Trust me, Andy."

He rolled his eyes. "Whatever. Pardon me if I'm not too

sensitive about her preferences at the moment. She's made it perfectly clear that she'll never forgive me for teaching you the gospel and showing you a better way to live."

I bit my tongue. Yes, he'd tried to do those things, but I wasn't sure how good of a student I had been. I was still a far cry from being as wholesome as the people my age I met at church. In fact, I was pretty sure that level of wholesomeness was completely lost to someone like me—no matter how hard I tried.

Andy was staring at the door again. "When I envisioned coming here, everything was different. I saw you with all these friends from your ward always calling and texting you. I saw a whole new start here, with a glow on your face and a light in your eye." He turned and his eyes focused on me. "But everything's the same as when I left you in California. Kay's here. You're dating a guy who won't be in good standing with the Church for at least another year—at best."

I had no answer for that, so I said nothing.

"My mom always says you can judge a person by their friends." He let the words hover between us as if it were my duty to deal with his interpretation of what his mom said.

Yeah, Kay was giving him a rough time, but that didn't mean he knew the first thing about her. And I had to agree with Kay when she said he obviously didn't want to even try to know her. Just the fact that he refused to call her Kathryn was proof of this.

Andy just wanted a pleasant visit, and so did I. What I did not want was for him to draw a line in the sand after less than twenty-four hours in my world.

"No comment?" he asked.

I moved to the kitchen for some water. The increased physical distance between us was just a bonus. "I asked her not to speak to you anymore." I pulled out glasses for both of us. "Sorry she's being mean. She just doesn't understand your motives."

This time Andy was the one who kept quiet. Once both glasses were filled, I walked over and handed him one. Our eyes met, and for the barest of moments, his eyes flickered south.

"When does Ty get off work?" he asked.

I blinked and stepped back.

"Whoa! That came out wrong," he backpedaled.

Had it? I glanced at the clock, choosing to ignore what had happened. "Actually, he's off now. Probably running errands or something." Or, if he had chosen to come home directly, he was about five minutes out. He didn't have his truck since he'd done the commute by foot that morning.

"You don't know what he's doing after work?" Andy asked. This seemed important to him.

"I make it a point not to stalk my boyfriend." And it was true. If I started down that rabbit hole, I would only fall deeper and deeper. It was good for me if I didn't know where Ty was for a full hour of a day. Granted, I could probably find him if I tried, but the point was that I didn't. It was that whole trust thing I'd developed with him somehow.

Andy's body language became deliberately casual. "You know it's my duty to vet any guys you date, right? We've got to make sure you find a guy worthy of you."

We? I forced myself to relax as I sat next to him. "Oh, Ty's worthy. I promise."

"Well, you're certainly compatible workout buddies. That box gets a check."

The validation had me relaxing a little. "Yes, we're physically compatible."

His jaw flexed and his eyes flashed a tiny second before he reclaimed his casual demeanor. "So, how long have you two been dating?"

"Technically? Four weeks." That seemed impossible, but it was true.

"Four weeks?" he echoed.

"Yeah, but I knew him for three months before then. We were friends first."

He nodded sagely. "So are the two of you exclusive?"

Oh, I'd made myself very clear on that front when I kissed Ty in the airport a month ago. When we'd broken apart, I'd looked him dead in the eye and said, *If you want to do that again, you'd better not even think about touching someone else.*

Ty's response had been to smile and kiss me again.

"Yes, we're exclusive." That one rule was hard and fast with me these days.

Andy's brow furrowed, and I let him have his little moment to process. If Kay and Ty were right about Andy having ulterior motives for hanging around, I needed to send as clear a message as I could. It was only fair.

"If I have my way, Andy, I'll marry Ty. And, really, I have you to thank for that. Without you I never would have met Ty."

He didn't smile as his thumb traced the rim of his water glass. "I just expected more for you, I guess."

He was dead serious.

"Are you kidding?" I asked. "Ty's phenomenal."

His eyes dropped, and he bit his bottom lip while still thumbing his glass. He took his time replying. "Where are your Mormon friends, Rhea? I've only see you in contact with two people. One's anti-Mormon and the other probably should have been excommunicated. I want you to have friends who lift you up, not drag you down."

The words were as shocking as a punch to the face.

"I mean, I've been here nearly a full day and you haven't mentioned the Church once. You did the tour at Temple Square with me, but I didn't see a light in your eyes as you listened. Then you took off the second you had an excuse."

He stared at me with the eyes that had so unapologetically taught me the missionary discussions. "Do you have a calling? Are you still going to church?"

"Yes," I snapped, unable to hide my annoyance.

"Then why don't I see the influence of God in your life here? Why are you dating a guy who can't take you to the temple? Why are you spending all your time with a supposed best friend who despises your beliefs? I appreciate that you have friends outside of the Church, but you need to make sure you don't let them inhibit your spiritual growth."

Whoa, whoa, and *whoa!* The effort it took to bite back what was on the tip of my tongue was monumental. Had he dared to look at me while saying all that, Andy would have seen the flash of fury in my eyes. Luckily for both of us, though, he only looked up from his glass after giving me a few beats to compose myself.

Then, as if someone had cued him for his entrance, I heard Ty's feet move up my front steps. He wasn't even going home to shower first? I guess I should thank him for that, because he was about to preemptively break up my first fight with Andy and grant me the time to create a carefully crafted response to Andy's bigoted wishes for me and my life.

Ty walked in, sweaty and hot, and, with a flare of annoyance, immediately noted me and Andy on the couch together. Seriously, his interpretation of the situation could not have been more off, but if I had walked in on him with a girl on a couch, I might have jumped to the same conclusions.

I stood and gave him a quick kiss, handing him my drink. "You made good time. Drink?"

"Please," he agreed, guzzling the water. Andy and I eyed each other.

"We were just talking about you," I said to Ty, my voice all innocence. "Andy was asking how long we've been dating."

Ty stopped drinking long enough to say. "Sounds like an interesting conversation. Sorry to interrupt." He wasn't.

"Also, Andy found the car he wants this morning," I added, and finally an authentic smile crossed Andy's face. "He may have a new car tomorrow."

"I just need approval on financing," he beamed.

"Sweet," Ty said, handing me the empty glass and perking up for car talk. "What are you getting?"

"A blue Mini Cooper," Andy said proudly.

Ty faltered, but only for a moment. "Not my style, but hey, good for you." The words weren't forced or fake, and I gripped Ty's hand to let him know I appreciated him not turning all guy on Andy and laughing. Although in that moment, I wouldn't feel too bad if Ty jabbed at Andy. One of us had to be mature, though.

"It's no Avalanche," Andy qualified. "But it fits my needs."

"Sure," Ty agreed.

That conversation finished, Ty and Andy had nothing to do but eye each other with equal wariness. An awkward tension filled the room. Par for the course since Andy showed up. The only difference was that this time I didn't care.

"I should probably take a shower," Ty said.

"Good idea. Can I walk you guys home?" It was a not-so-subtle hint in Andy's direction. Being separated from him for a while would do me some good. Ty nodded and Andy set his glass down on the coffee table.

The smile on Ty's face as we walked out of my house did not go unnoticed by me. He knew I was mad at Andy for some reason, which seemed to improve his mood.

"So what's on the slate tonight?" he asked as we crossed my yard. I glanced at him in surprise.

"Aren't you teaching gymnastics?" Yes, the guy did gymnastics on top of everything else. If I ever fell out of love with Ty, all he'd need was about ten whole seconds of a ring routine to make my heart go pitter-patter again. So hot. And he taught a class twice a week.

"Found a sub, so I'm all yours tonight."

"We could hike or something," I offered. "Andy and I don't

have anything specific planned."

"I was thinking of meeting up with some old mission buddies, actually," Andy chimed in, earning a surprised look from both me and Ty. "I should be getting a call soon to finalize our plans."

The corner of Ty's mouth tilted up as he sent me a sly look. "Sounds fun. That means I get you all to myself, babe."

"Whatever shall we do?" I asked.

Andy rolled his eyes and walked faster until he was running up Ty's front steps and pulling out his phone.

"In a way, you've got to feel bad for him," Ty mused as Andy walked through the front door and out of earshot.

"No, I don't," I said, sounding too much like Kay. "If you would have walked in five seconds later, he and I would have been in a messy fight."

He nodded. "I sensed that. What did he do?"

My pulse picked up at the mere memory. "He thinks I should have friends more righteous than you and Kay."

To my surprise, Ty chuckled. "I don't envy the guy. Like I said last night, he's going to be weird for a while."

"Maybe forever?" I added.

"Maybe. But hey, at least he's buying a Mini Cooper," he said, chuckling in disbelief. "That's such a chick car. I could totally see you driving one around town, but no way could you ride shotgun with your man."

"For the hundredth time, Ty, it's not like that with Andy!"

"Oh, I see that now. I was just nervous when you showed me the pictures of him on Facebook. Not that I make it habit of checking out guys, but he's not bad looking."

"No, he's not," I agreed. "He'll have girls stalking him at school, for sure."

He stopped and faced me. "As long as you're not one of them, that's fine by me."

"Not in a million years," I promised, hoping for a kiss until I noticed Ty's focus move behind me as he frowned slightly.

"Do you need help?" he called over my shoulder, and I turned to see his neighbor unloading a massive plant from the back of her Subaru.

"Oh, I should be fine," his neighbor called back, but both of us were already walking over as she bent her voluptuous body over at the waist and hefted a massive spider plant.

LeAnna Broadhead: married, two children, thirteen traffic violations, 580 credit score, and a Chapter 13 in 2003 that forced all credit requests, including the mortgage of the house, into her husband's name. She also had a little bit of a neighbor crush on Ty, as evidenced by her slight blush when she looked at him. But it was innocent, and as long as I didn't find her and Ty "sharing a couch," I was fine with it.

"How many plants do you have in there?" Ty asked as we drew closer. Her rear seats were folded down, and she had filled the entire car with house plants lined up vase to vase.

"My sister's business moved," she explained, looking embarrassed. "They were just going to throw all these in a dumpster."

Ty looked at the orphan plants with new regard. "Well, look at you playing Robin Hood."

"Want one?" she offered. "Or five? You too, Rhea. I have no idea where I'm going to put them all. If you really want to help carry them in, just inside in the living room would be great. Easier to give away that way."

"Sure," Ty said, grabbing the massive pot she'd been struggling with in one hand and snatching another plant before carrying them both in. For a moment, LeAnna just watched him walk.

"Bless my husband's heart, but he never had arms like that," she pined. She sent me a knowing look. "You've got a keeper there."

"Tell me about it," I agreed, grabbing a pot as well.

She let out a weary sigh. "Thanks for helping me. It wore me out just packing all these in, to tell the truth."

"Of course!" I said, heading to the house. "Glad to."

Ty was on his way back when I walked in the house. I was looking for a place to put the raphis in my hands when my eyes fell on something unexpected: an open laptop.

My steps stilled as I regarded the laptop and its potential.

This morning, Oliver Westman had made it very clear that I was under surveillance. For the past eight hours, I'd followed orders because no viable opportunity to disobey them had presented itself. Mark Epson was off limits, and if I so much as Googled his name on my computer, red flags would pop up all over the bad guys' radar. But what if I did it on another computer, off radar, and logged in under someone else's account? My old coworkers would never know. No, it wasn't technically legal, but whatever was going on with Mark Epson was just as illegal.

Terrified at the direction of my thoughts, I put the plant down and hustled back out to the car. Too late: the laptop was all I could think of now.

Running away from temptation, I flashed Ty and LeAnna a vacant smile as I hustled back to the car to grab two overgrown snake plants.

My pulse had picked up. Not a good sign. The adrenaline pumped through me filled me with false courage that had my mind plotting how to get on LeAnna's computer. If I hurried, I could walk into the house right behind her . . . which was what I was doing. I was going to do it!

What was wrong with me?

Not allowing myself to consider my motives, I stopped beside her to make room for Ty as he moved past us back to the car. LeAnna and I walked into the living room.

"My, this room is filling up quickly, isn't it?" she said.

"Should I just put these on the coffee table?" I offered.

Right next to your open laptop?

"Sure," she agreed. "Wherever you can. It's a good thing we're almost done!"

I set the spider plants down and pointedly looked at her laptop. "LeAnna?" I said and pointed to the laptop when she looked my way. "Do you mind?" I had to be careful how I asked to use it in the off chance that what we were saying could be heard.

"Of course!" she replied. "Feel free!"

I wanted to hug her for not mentioning the computer by name and didn't waste a second hopping on.

"Take your time," she said, heading back out to the car.

Unfortunately, taking my time wasn't an option. I needed info and I needed it fast. Who was Mark Epson and who cared?

Logging into Utah Courts, I learned that Mark had nothing like a spotless record. Far from it, in fact. He'd even been charged with a few felonies back in the day but pled down in court. I got excited until I saw what his felonies were. He'd been caught naked in public a few times—once on top of the University of Utah's library.

There had to be a story behind that.

Curious as to what kind of woman married an exhibitionist, I looked up Julie Epson. No records. Not even a ticket.

Uh-uh. No way. No one was that perfect. Not even my perfect ex-boyfriend, Chad. Perfection was suspicious in my book. Especially when it married a guy who got caught with his pants down on the rooftops of public buildings.

The more I sped read through Mark's case files, the more I wanted to meet him.

I didn't have time to do a full search, so I stuck with the basics: his social, his address history, and his finances.

Using the info provided from Utah Courts, I opened a

new tab in my browser and logged into another site that would give me all that info in one search. Thirty seconds never felt so long as it generated the report. Ty walked in and furrowed his eyebrows in an amused look. When he opened his mouth to speak, I shook my head.

"Just arranging stuff in here," I said innocently. "How many more plants are there?"

My words confused him, as they would anyone, but after a short pause he said, "Oh, one more trip and we're good."

"Great. Put the rest on the piano."

"Sounds good," he said a little too loudly. He then mouthed, *What's going on?*

I shook my head again and motioned toward the door for him to leave. *Later.*

Good boyfriend that he is, he walked right back outside.

When I looked back down, Mark's report lay in front of me. I quickly memorized his social security number, noting that he was a Utah native. He came from a family of all boys, which might explain his bizarre, and likely competitive, behavior. He and his wife had a house in their name two blocks from the university with no mortgage on it. Pretty unusual for two people barely breaking thirty, but that might be explained by the store the couple owned and operated. The numbers I was seeing didn't exactly show them as being in the poor house.

I scanned the rest of the report, tucking the information away in hopes that it would be available for recall, if needed. As I neared the end, LeAnna walked in.

"Is that thing working okay for you?"

Time was up. "Yep!" I said, keeping my voice peppy as I indicated her new plants with my eyes. "You've got some nice, durable plants here. It should be easy to find them homes."

"From your mouth to God's ears," she said, looking around at her new jungle. "What was I thinking?"

"You were thinking that you know people who can't afford

plants but would love to have these in their home." I logged out, clearing my search history in the browser and off the hard drive. At the last minute I decided to change the IP address, just in case. If someone came in here looking to see if I had been on the computer, they would figure it out if they sniffed around, but I didn't have to make it obvious.

"Virginia," she said with a nod. "I know she would love that one." She pointed to the raphis.

I shut the laptop. "Well, I'm glad you let us help."

Ty stepped through the door with the last two plants. "On the piano?" he asked.

"Perfect," LeAnna said. "Thank you two so much. I'll need to invite you over to dinner."

"Not necessary," I said, suddenly nervous. Now was not the time to make friends. Not when rich hit men were allegedly watching me.

"Do you have a new roommate, Ty?" she asked. "I saw another handsome young man around your house last night."

"No," Ty said without hesitation.

"He's my friend," I confessed. "He's starting school at BYU soon, and Ty's just letting him stay while he gets settled."

"Oh?" She perked up like the neighborhood gossip she was. "That sounds . . . interesting."

I shrugged. "Not really, but we do need to get back to him. Anything else we can do?"

"No, no," she said quickly. "Get on your way. And thanks again for your help."

"Anytime," Ty said as I subtly pulled him out the door. His face held the same bewilderment that it had when he'd caught me on the laptop, so I cut him off before he could ask any questions.

"I hope Andy's mission friends can pick him up tonight," I said, pulling him toward his house.

"Me too." He drew me into a not-so-hurried kiss. When

he decided he was done, he moved his mouth to my ear and whispered with impossible softness, "You've *so* got to tell me what's going on."

Stepping away, I gave a playful slap to his chest. "Oh Ty, you're such a tease."

My response made no sense, which was the point. If I wrote it in neon letters across the sky, could I be any more obvious that I did not want to talk about it?

To my relief, he laughed. "Fine, then. We can go see a movie." He was playing the game with me. To show him my relief, I went up on my toes and gave him a quick peck.

"You decide. You're the one playing hookey."

A mischievous glint popped in his eye. "I'll do that. But first let's make sure we're really alone tonight."

ELEVEN

TY HADN'T BEEN kidding when he mentioned the movie. Once Andy was out the door, Ty threw a mattress in the back of his truck and drove me to the drive-in for some entertainment à la Pixar.

The boy was full of surprises, considering seeing a movie was something we usually avoided like a rash.

I watched traffic the entire way. No one followed us. When we arrived and parked, Ty blasted the radio as we hopped into the back of his truck. The outdoor movie screen blocked the sunset and provided shade to a group of tailgaters sitting in beanbag chairs and eating hotdogs.

"Wow, I didn't know Utah had a ghetto," I said, leaning against the cab and watching six kids all try to fit on the same chair.

He chuckled. "Welcome to the west side, Jensen."

I narrowed my eyes at him. I didn't like it when he called me by my last name, and he knew it. Which was why he did it—to make sure he had my attention.

His location for the date may have been less classy than usual, but I saw Ty's genius in bringing me here. As he filled the space next to me on the mattress, he whispered, "At last, we get to talk."

Eyeing the fifty cars around us, with their dozens of conversations and stereos competing to be heard while everyone waited for the movie to start, I smiled. No technology I knew of could filter through all that noise and listen in.

Sending him a doting look, I sighed dramatically. "I love dating you. Have I said that recently?"

"Nope. Now spill."

I paused, not because I wasn't going to tell him, but because I was. How much had life changed in the past six months that I would even consider confiding the details of my situation in someone without hesitation? I'd never done it with Ben and rarely with Kay. And even earlier today, I'd only given her broad strokes.

And I was about to tell Ty everything.

Starting from the beginning, I laid it out for him. When the previews came on, Ty jumped back into the cab to change the channel to match the screen, but then hopped back in and draped an arm around me as I finished the story, including what I had done at LeAnna's. When I was finished, I actually felt better. Stronger.

How was that possible?

For several beats, he appeared to be watching the movie as if I'd said nothing important at all. "So is your old boss in the Mafia, or something?" he asked at last.

"Not Mafia," I answered, feeling pretty certain about that. "Something else, but not Mafia."

He shook his head. "Your life is never boring, is it?"

"Not most days," I agreed, and we fell silent.

"Kay will figure it out," he said at last. "Everything will work out if you keep out of it. That's probably best."

"Yeah." We grew silent, pretending that was the end of that conversation when we both knew it wasn't.

"I heard Andy on the phone with his dad," he said. "It sounds like the purchase is going down tomorrow. The kid will officially have his own wheels."

"Nice." And it would be. Autonomy would be good for me and Andy. Too much togetherness time didn't suit us.

"I'm sorry."

I looked at him, confused. "Sorry about what?"

"That you're seeing he's not the perfect missionary you thought he was. We're all human."

I turned to the screen so I wouldn't have to look at him. "I know that."

"Yeah, but sometimes we're seem little more superhuman when we're playing a role," he mused. "Missionaries live a strict life with defined goals and no distractions. When you put on that tag, you have only one purpose—to represent Christ." He looked away. "When you lose that mantle, things get confusing pretty quickly."

"He's a twenty-one-year-old guy. I get that. I'm not asking him to be more." Or was I?

Ty's eyes met mine again. "Don't get me wrong. I hate that he's trying to steal you, but since I know he's going to fail, I can pity him a little."

I laughed outright. "You're sure?"

"Oh, yeah. No question." He leaned in for a kiss, which I surrendered without a fight. It was one of the few I would get that night, which was kind of a bummer. But it also made me feel safe.

If there was one thing I could do, it was trust Ty. And that felt unspeakably good.

"I think we're supposed to be watching the movie," he said when he pulled away.

"Then turn your head," I replied. And he did.

TWELVE

I COULDN'T SLEEP THAT night. Conversations with Kay, Ty, and especially Andy were swimming in my head. But most of all, there was Mark Epson, the quasi-innocent guy who'd been framed as a suicide jumper.

Since when was I one to be bribed off a case?

My mind played the scene with Oliver Westman and his companion over and over, picking up new details and letting them fester.

Yes, they had money. Yes, they had backing, but had I been giving them too much credit when it came to their capabilities? Were they simply overconfident men who figured that showing up on my doorstep would be enough to scare me into inaction?

The thought that I might have fallen for scare tactics pretty much made my blood boil. Back in L.A., there was no way I would have sat on a threat like that for an entire nineteen hours. But here? When I was in love and had a friend who'd just taken a dive in her career for me? Those things made me soft.

Regardless, it was time to find out exactly what I was dealing with.

Sneaking out my own bedroom window, I slipped through the shadows into the shed I'd built in my backyard. Instead of your typical garden rakes and shovels, it housed my surveillance equipment and a small arsenal. And yes, it took more than a key to open it.

The shed was dark when I slid in, and I kept it that way until the door was completely shut behind me. Only then did I reach up and pull the lamp string.

Tonight was a night for counter-surveillance gear; I needed to know how heavily I was being watched. Of course, shotgun and long-distance mics were nearly impossible to trace, but I could jam those with a scrambling device if I wanted.

Moving through my shelves, I picked up a variety of tools that would help me diagnose what kind of a situation Oliver and Company had put me in: a laser scanner, audio jammer, and a couple of silent bug detectors for my phone and computer to see if information was being duplicated.

Pulling the light back off, I slipped back into the shadows, crossed the yard, and climbed back into my room.

The first gadget on my list was a specific type of laser scanner. It was time to find out how much I was overreacting. How many cameras, if any, were in my home?

No matter what form a camera takes, it always has a lens. And lenses reflect light. When my laser sent out its broad pulse, I should have been able to locate lenses as a pinpoint of red light reflecting back at me, making them easy to spot.

There were no cameras in my bedroom. None in my bathroom, either. I guess I should be grateful for that. I moved through the house, making sure my steps were silent, and found nothing.

No cameras.

Still feeling uneasy, I moved out to my car with both the camera detector and the bug detector and slid into the driver's seat. The light from the laser scanner was a lot brighter in an enclosed space, but at last it revealed a faint reflection in my dome light. Knowing the laser could just be reflecting off the bulb inside, I removed the plastic cover and was totally rewarded for my efforts.

Inside the dome, aimed toward the street, was an itsy bitsy camera, but no microphone transmitter that I could see.

There had to be a mic.

If they had a camera in my car, they had an audio transmitter somewhere. I searched with my second device, knowing that a mic could be turned off at will when the surveillance party had no use for it.

Leaving the camera where it was, I replaced the dome cover and went back inside the house.

No cameras in the house and one in the car. When I was driving, they saw what I saw, until I wanted to change the game. Good to know.

I took a second turn around the house, looking for mics, and again came up empty. Either there was nothing there, or nothing was broadcasting at the moment. I'd have to do it again during daylight hours. These guys knew my schedule and were probably asleep right now, waiting for me to get up at five.

Or was I giving them too much credit again?

It was time to lay questions like that to rest.

Sitting on the floor of my living room, I closed my eyes and took a breath to focus. These guys belonged to the same group Elliott did, and Elliott had trained me. That had to give me a leg up on their tactics. All I had to do was recall the beginning of my career, when I had followed Elliott's direction with precision. Over the years, I had developed my own strategies and let some of his teachings fall by the wayside.

Alone in the dark, with the clock clicking toward three in the morning, I thought back six years. It was hard to focus when I thought back that far. Every memory seemed to have Kay, Ben, and other friends featured, derailing me on a trip down memory lane as I drifted to sleep. It took conscious effort to keep my thoughts where they would be helpful.

How to hide in plain sight and when to hide completely. How to pick a pocket and plant a bug. How to scale fences and navigate in the dark. Those were the basic lessons. I'd mostly practiced on Ben and his friends in the beginning. Without them, I never would have perfected the art of slipping in and out of people's personal spaces.

In the beginning, the cases had all been glamorous. Maybe Elliott planned it that way to keep my attention, or maybe I just had the right look to blend in. Either way, he'd taught me how to infiltrate people's worlds. Gadgets, toys, and electronic surveillance were all prized tools in his box, but I ended up dropping most of them after awhile. They stressed me out and made me less observant. Plus, they were too easy for me to lose and others to find.

But pinpointing when Elliott and I parted ways wasn't the point of rifling through my memories; I still needed to figure out how some of his cohorts were watching me now.

They'd dropped me an envelope with fifty grand. A courtesy payment, nigh unto an insult. They thought they were better than me. If I were them, I'd place a few strategic bugs and trackers and call it good, unless the subject raised some red flags. It was the treatment typically given to a co-subject in Elliott's model of surveillance. It meant I was number two on their list. Or lower.

Who was number one? Mark Epson? Someone else entirely? For the moment it didn't matter. They had likely only planted a single bug on me, and just like Elliott would have done, they would have done so in a different place than the camera. They'd want it in a place where they could hear me at all times, which would mean they would want it physically on me. The problem with that was there was nothing I wore so consistently that they could—

Wow. I was totally blind.

We all have things we wear every day out of habit. A

ring, a watch, or a necklace. Some people can't bear to have their cell phone more than arm's distance away. I had none of those things, but I did have what Kay called my ninja bracelet. Armed with a dozen different trade tools that came in handy in a pinch, it was my security blanket and good luck charm.

And I was betting my hush money that it now housed a bug. That's absolutely where Elliott would have planted a bug if he were watching me, and conveniently, the bracelet housed plenty of hiding places.

Had it seriously taken me twenty hours to figure that out?

The good news was that I now knew where the bug was and didn't need to tip them off by looking for it. Even better news was that I could jam the signal whenever I wanted. The best news was that I had a lot more freedom than I originally thought. This might actually be fun.

Unless they were serious about their threat on hurting people. I had to make sure I gave them no ammo to follow through with that threat.

Too amped to sleep, I went back to bed anyway and waited for my alarm to go off.

THIRTEEN

TWO HOURS LATER, Ty let himself in my front door and padded down to the basement. Yesterday we ran, so today was combat training. My eyes moved behind Ty after I kissed him hello.

"No Andy this time," he said with a grin. "He got in late and went straight to bed."

I hated that I was relieved as I turned on the music. Adrenaline would have to take me through this workout since my body hadn't done any resting, but it would make it. And then some. I had quite a day planned for myself, and it all started with stretching.

Forty-five minutes later, Ty ducked out to get ready for work, and I went for a little run up to the university to get a look at the Epsons' house. For this I took another of Elliott's toys that I hadn't used in at least a year—a different laser scanner that created 3-D models of what you programmed it to map. The scanner was large enough that I had to hide it in my Camelbak, but the day might come when I broke into the Epsons, and I wanted to know what I was dealing with when I did.

Within five minutes of the Epsons' home being in sight, I was leaving it behind with a full map of the structure ready to be uploaded to my computer. Things felt right again. I had a plan.

And if things went well, no one would get hurt. All I had to do was stay under the radar until I was ready to make my move.

Life was easier when opposition underestimated you, but the past twenty-four hours had taught me a good lesson. It was better to take my approach and test my enemy than do what Oliver had chosen to do and treat me as an afterthought.

I'd much rather be in my shoes than his.

Upon arriving home, I took a shower, put on my bracelet, and did my usual routine of checking news feeds online. I kept everything normal—boring, even. At about eight, I called Andy, who answered with an artificial amount of pep in his voice.

"Good morning!"

"Morning," I replied with equal oomph. "You ready to get a car today?"

"Totally! Can I steal a ride over?"

"I was planning on it," I agreed.

"Thanks, Rhea. It means a lot."

Something had changed while he was with his friends the night before. I could sense it. Whatever it was, I would probably hear about it sometime during the day. Until then, we both seemed content to exchange niceties. We made plans to head over to the dealership at nine, which gave me just enough time to pack a bag full of toys and change into some clothes that attract the right attention.

As I tossed the bag into my trunk and shut the lid, my phone buzzed with a text. Kay, of course. My life was just that predictable.

Feeling left in the cold yet? Tag, you're it.

Ah, Kay. The girl was being sneaky and had guessed that the text would be read by someone besides me. We only "tagged" each other when we were giving the other a leg up, which meant she had something for me . . . in the cold. And since nothing was cold in Utah right now, I had to assume she left whatever she was talking about in her freezer.

The day before, I would have been too paranoid to try to retrieve anything she stashed for me, but today I knew better. With a few gadgets and a little diversion, I would be in the clear to sneak in and out of Kay's. I had a key to her house, just like she had a key to mine.

I don't mind the cold, I texted back. *Good luck!* It was best to keep her in the dark while I figured out what we were dealing with.

* * *

An hour later, it was raining paperwork at the Mini dealership. It would have been a perfect time to slip out, were it not for the distance of the dealership from Kay's place. It was a solid twelve-mile round trip, which would take too long on foot.

Sitting next to Andy in front of the loan officer's desk while the man convinced Andy's dad on the speaker phone that Andy's new baby needed undercoating to protect against the salt on Utah's roads, I typed a note out on my phone and showed it to Andy. *I'm going to step out for about 20 minutes. That cool?*

Andy read it and nodded, looking a little overwhelmed at all the details he was being forced to muddle through. I grabbed my driver's license from my wallet and left my purse where it was. I'd already removed my bracelet and placed it in my purse to pick up the conversation, in case anyone was masochistic enough to listen to contract details. Just to be safe, I also left my phone as I slid out the door and headed toward a salesman who I'd noticed looking at me more than once. His name tag said Matt.

"Hi," I said with a little flirt in my eye.

His eyes involuntarily looked me over before he could stop them. "Hey."

I hesitated, checking his left hand for a ring. There was

nothing there, but I swear he'd looked at me like a married man would. "So, my friend in there says Minis are the only way to go."

This time his eyes moved to my Audi in the customer parking. "Well, they're great, but they may not be a step up for you."

I pursed my lips and nodded my agreement. "Still, mind if I take one for a test drive and find out?"

"No problem," he agreed. "Let me grab some keys."

"A convertible," I decided. Why not? "The K3679."

He appraised me with new eyes. "Looks like someone was paying attention."

"I try." He was flirting. I was flirting. And if Ty were there, he'd be clenching his fists. I mentally took note of that, even as I chose not to care. I did what needed to be done. This wasn't personal. I just needed him cooperative.

I waited in the lobby for the possibly married salesman to return with my ride. When he did, he was all charm.

"We're headed for the yellow one, third from the entrance."

"Nice." He fell into step beside me, walking just a hair too close. "I've got to warn you that I feel it's my duty to test this car out a bit," I said.

He chuckled, full of confidence. "I'm sure this car can take anything you choose to dish out."

If so, I'd have to buy one, but that probably wasn't going to happen. Little cars were death traps when something went wrong.

"We'll see," I said as I changed the subject so Matt could fall into sales mode while I took him downtown. He probably would have taken the drive with me downtown whether I slid him coy looks or not, but it was all kind of second nature for me. Besides, Ty worked it for the ladies who came into train.

I'd watched Ty flirt a time or two, spotting when it wasn't

necessary and maintaining eye contact a little too long. Would a time come when he would stop doing that? After all, as I had clearly pointed out to Andy, Ty and I had only been dating for a month. Were Ty and I at the "no flirting with others for personal gain" point of our relationship?

I'd have to ask later. Like in another month . . . or six. Stereotypically, girls moved faster than guys in relationships. Ty liked me—wanted me, even—but he didn't know enough about me to have a serious commitment in mind.

Occupational flirting without intent was still allowed. I was decreeing it so. And not just because it served me at the moment. Any flirting with intent, however, was completely off the menu. That I also decreed. I'd have to inform Ty later, when I didn't have a guy pretending to casually rest his arm on the door of a Mini Cooper to show me his flexed bicep. His arms were okay, but the ones I'd grown accustomed to having around me were far superior.

The convertible top made talking a little more difficult once we got on the freeway. When he motioned to the next exit, yelling over the wind to take it, I very purposefully ignored him and zipped on. The little thing did have its fair share of juice. Stunt driving in it would be a blast.

"Take I-80 to State," he said as we moved to the next exit. I shook my head.

"Downtown," I called back. "I've got to show this to someone." Then I smiled one of those spoiled-rotten, reckless smiles of a girl used to getting her way and floored it.

Matt gripped the door and the dash as I pushed the car up to 100 miles an hour and wove through the light, midday traffic. We got to the downtown exit much too soon, and I slowed down for the off-ramp.

"Nice!" Matt called as we slowed, but I knew he was nervous. Wrecking on a test drive would probably mean a lot of paperwork for him.

"Thanks," I said, brushing my hair out of my face. "I have a friend who needs to see this. She's, like, a mile away." I didn't ask, and Matt didn't object.

"Is she as hot as you?" he asked.

I could say whatever I wanted since Kay wasn't home, but I stuck with the truth. "Hotter." He liked it. Worked for me.

Thanks to well-timed traffic lights, we were in front of Kay's new condo in under three minutes. I pulled over into a truck unloading zone and left the car running.

"Be right back," I said to Matt, and moved to the entrance. Reaching into my pocket, I pulled out my jammer and flipped it on. Security was minimal at Kay's condo, but it did have cameras. What were the chances of Oliver and Company tapping into those and watching Kay's lobby? Basically none, but I wasn't one to be caught because I took the lazy route.

I crossed the lobby in a casual walk and hit the elevator button to go up. Out on the street, Matt stayed in the passenger seat and checked his watch. Then he moved the rearview mirror to check his teeth, prepping for his hot date.

If it turned out Matt was married, I was going to have to think up something fun for him. Kay would help. She'd have to be careful because she was on TV, but she still had some tricks up her sleeve. And she hated guys who weren't faithful.

The elevator dinged and opened up to let me in. I hit the fifth floor and headed up. Walk in, check the freezer, get out. If there was nothing there, I had just wasted a trip. No harm, no foul.

Using my key, I let myself in her front door, walked through her meticulous entry, and turned for the kitchen. Her freezer held nothing but edemame and black bean burgers, so I moved to the fridge, and voila: a folder about a half-inch thick. I was usually the one providing her with info like this, so it was weird to have the tables turned.

Snatching it, I headed back out the door and locked it

behind me, tucking the folder in the back of my pants. I should have just told Matt I was making a business stop with his car. It would have been just as easy and explained why I was walking out with a folder.

Oh, well.

I took the stairs down to ground level, one hand in my pocket until I walked out the front door, where I turned off the jammer. Matt looked behind me and waited until I got a little closer before he asked, "Where's your friend?"

"Not here," I said with a shrug and ran back around to the driver's seat. "Total bummer. She'd love this car." Kay would hate it. She was married to her hybrid and the hope of alternative energy in the next decade. I was all for alternative energy too, but in the meantime I was going to work with what I had.

"You'll have to bring her in. I'll give you a card so that she knows to ask for me."

I put the car in drive. "I'll do that." I smiled, kind of hoping that there was a Mrs. Matt. "Think I can get us back in eight minutes?"

"Uh, no." His voice was firm, indicating he didn't want me to try.

"Well, you're no fun," I pouted, and pulled into traffic.

* * *

Andy was the proud owner of a brand new, horizon blue Mini Cooper with white accent racing stripes and a carbon black interior. Watching him circle it like a worried parent while I lay on the grass of my front lawn was kind of fun. He kept running a polishing rag over it again and again.

He let his hand hover where he'd just polished. "I want to take a road trip, but I don't want any dirt to get on it."

"Oh, it's going to get dirty," I said, soaking in the afternoon sun. "Might as well have some memories getting it that way. Take it up the canyon or down to Provo to check out the city. You're going to be living there, after all."

His face became somber. "Yeah."

Not the reaction I had been expecting. "You not excited to start in January?"

"It's not that," he said quickly. He looked at me and not in a good way. "I just—"

Great. We were about to "talk."

He let out a heavy sigh. "I just don't want to leave you here like this."

I looked around, wondering what he saw, because as far as I was concerned, I was pretty set. "Like what?"

He leaned against the Cooper, arms folded and tense. "You're my convert, Rhea. It's my job to make sure you grow in the gospel." He was dead serious.

I leveraged myself up to my elbows. "Andy, you've been released. You're not a missionary anymore." Was that the right thing to say? Had anyone ever said it to him? I wasn't sure. I imagined Ty cringing if he were a fly on the wall. I probably could have said it better.

"I know that, Rhea, but—"

But what?

"I wish I could see evidence of the gospel in your life, that's all. I wish you had a picture of the temple or Christ in your home. I wish you were excited about some single's activity this weekend. Things like that."

What could I say to that? "Sorry."

"But Ty has me worried the most," he confessed, starting to fidget with his polishing rag. "I want you to be with a man who can marry you in the temple."

This was getting into awfully personal territory, but I felt I should respond. "I don't plan on getting married in the temple, Andy." I held up my hand to hush his knee-jerk reaction. "I plan on getting sealed, sure, but you have to understand. It's just me and my dad, and he's been planning my wedding day since the day I was born. You should see his yard, Andy. It could be the eighth world wonder, and he keeps it that way in part because he wants the perfect stage for my wedding."

"But it's not forever!" he shot back.

"I *know* it's not," I said softly. "But getting married without my dad there is not something that's going to happen. Ever."

"But—"

"I've been a member of the Church for four months, Andy. If you ask me, I've made some remarkable changes in that time. But where and how I get married will not be one of them. If my dad could come into the temple, then I'd consider it. And the thing is, I can have it both ways. It's the Church that makes me choose between it and my dad, and I'm not righteous enough to choose the Church in that situation. That's just how it is, whether Ty's in the picture or not, Andy."

He really didn't like that.

"My dad, my aunts, my uncles, and cousins. Kay, old friends, and coworkers. That's who I want to witness me getting married. Not a bunch of people I've only known a few months. Sorry, Andy. I'll get married in my dad's gardens, and then I'll be sealed a year later, when the Church will let me. That's the plan."

"It's a mistake," he grumbled.

"Well, then, it's a mistake I've chosen to make. It is in no way a reflection of how good of a missionary you were."

His eyes dropped to the rag in his hands. "I just can't help but think . . . "

Again, he didn't finish his sentence, and I wasn't going to do it for him.

"I talked about you last night with my mission friends." This was not a news flash. "One of the sisters thinks I have a crush on you and that I just want an excuse for you to break up with Ty."

That's what Ty thought too, but I knew more was coming when Andy pushed away from the car and sat down next to me.

"She was kind of right. Before I came to Salt Lake, I wondered if there was a reason I found you in L.A. There was something there. You sensed it, right?"

Thinking back, I had to admit that I'd felt something unique with Andy, but it had never been attraction. "Yes, there was something different about you."

He nodded, gaining courage. "When Elder Gonzales and I walked up to you and I saw your face for the first time, it literally took my breath away. It's why Elder Gonzales opened. He usually didn't with people like you—"

"People like me?" I interrupted. "What's that mean?"

His mouth fell open, empty of an answer for a moment. "You know . . . white . . . privileged. I usually did better opening with them."

"I see."

"It's not a racial thing," he defended quickly. "At least not on our side. A lot of white people claimed not to understand Gonzales when he spoke and just walked off."

"Then they clearly weren't the people you were looking for," I huffed.

"Be that as it may," he said, "when you talk to several hundred people a day, getting treated like that wears on you, so I took white people while I was with Gonzales, and he took Hispanic."

"Got it." It was none of my business anyway. Andy didn't need to justify anything to me.

"The point is, when I saw you, I forgot how to speak for a moment. That's never happened before." He paused. "Or since."

That was a lie, which I would normally let slide, but something told me not to. "Not even once?"

His eyes met mine, his mouth open to deny before he reconsidered. His eyes dipped down and to the right, remembering.

"When else has it happened?" I prompted.

His body flushed. I didn't see it, but even in the afternoon heat, I could feel the warmth wafting off him. He licked his lips, not knowing he did so. He was thinking of a girl, and I hoped it wasn't me.

"We're just friends," he said, more to himself than me.

"We, who?"

He turned to me, his eyes only half-seeing. "It's just too weird if we're more than friends. Isn't it?"

"Depends," I hedged. "Who is she?"

His mouth fell open. It did that a lot. His future wife better think it was adorable. "Sister Green."

Not me! Beautiful. I could so work with this.

"Would this be the same sister who accused you of being in love with me?"

Looking confused, he nodded his head.

"Then there's a good chance she's jealous. I say move forward and see what's there."

He visibly cringed. "With a sister missionary?"

"With a sister missionary," I affirmed. "Remember, neither of you are missionaries anymore."

"But I was her district leader!"

" 'Was' being the operative term, Andy. Now you're a hot guy with a six-pack who drives a Mini Cooper. She just might be into that."

He blushed. "I don't have anything to offer. Not yet," he confided, sounding like any twenty-one-year-old guy should. "It'll be at least six years before I graduate with my law degree. Until then, I'm just going to be a poor student."

I motioned to the car. "I promise you, Andy, there are poorer out there. You have no excuse not to take a girl out."

"I wasn't thinking dating," he said, sounding offended. For a moment I was confused until I saw that he was actually thinking about . . . yes, he was thinking about marriage! He hadn't even been out with this girl once, and he was trying to imagine being married to her.

Holy crap.

"Slow down there, tiger," I said, backing away from him a little bit. "You've got to kiss the girl first. Take the girl out to dinner, go grocery shopping with her, things like that. You don't even know if you're compatible."

"It's always been so easy to talk to her," he said, lost in his own world. "We'd always sit next to each other at meetings. It just felt natural."

Somebody needed to hit the brakes with this guy. "Andy?"

"And when she mentioned last night that she thought I might be in love with you, I knew the moment the words came out of her mouth that I wasn't. Not with you. But I couldn't say it because I couldn't stop looking at the annoyance in her eyes and wondering if she was jealous. I *wanted* her to be jealous!"

"So what are you going to do about it?"

He looked at me as if seeing me for the first time and grimaced. "This is a weird conversation to be having with you."

I shrugged. "And yet, I'm handy. Do you know where she is right now?"

"At school," he said without even a moment of thought. "She goes to the Y too."

"Also handy." In more ways than one. The drive took forty-five minutes each way. Kay's folder still sat in my backpack, unread.

"She's into botany. She wants to be a master gardener."

"I like her already." I'd grown up with plants. Nothing better for a kid, in my book.

"You know the weirdest thing about this?" he breathed.

"It's really not that weird. I know people will think it is when I tell them. The other elders will totally tease me, but I don't care."

"That's good."

He bit his bottom lip, fidgeting with the rag again. "Should I call her?"

"No!" I said a little too quickly. "Just drive down there. Let her know you're serious. Use the excuse of showing her your new car and then ask her if you can take her for a ride. She'll love it."

"Holy cow. This isn't happening."

That comment threw me off a bit. What wasn't happening? Him asking a girl on a date? Or was he planning on proposing at some point during the night? I honestly wasn't sure.

"Well, nothing's going to happen if you stay here sitting next to me."

He sent me a sly look. "We're not done talking about you, you know. Just because you've made me admit I have a crush on Marissa doesn't let you off the hook."

Bummer. "We'll deal with that another time, then. For now, get off your butt and go take your new wheels on a first drive to remember. If you two do end up together, it will be a very romantic detail."

"That's true!" he beamed. "I pretty much have to now, don't I?"

I nodded. "Pretty much."

"I need to change," he muttered and jogged off to Ty's, probably to put on another one of his outfits. Hopefully Marissa liked American Outfitters as well as Mini Coopers.

But that wasn't my problem. It was time to get Kay's folder and take a look at what she wanted to share with me. Should I do it at home? The library? A park? Oh, the options.

Might as well stick with home, since I knew it was clean. Inside, they would only hear me talk, which would do them no good when I was reading. After mine and Andy's heart-to-heart, hopefully they were too bored to be listening at all.

After grabbing the bag from behind my seat, where the camera couldn't see it, I went inside and down to my workout room. Sitting down in the middle of my judo mat, I took the folder out of the bag and flipped it open. To my surprise, the top page was handwritten by Kay.

> *Hi. I'm staying late to write this, FYI. All I know is that you always seem to know what people are typing at work, so these guys who have you spooked might be able to do the same. Hence, you have to endure my handwriting.*
>
> *The papers I'm including in this will be of interest to you. I know you're wondering where I got them. It pains me to say it, but I flirted them away from Officer Dahl with damsel talk. Ugh. Now I owe him twice, and he only owes me once. Hate that. That said, these papers better be worth something.*
>
> *You'll see that Mark Epson has been the head of a co-ed underground secret society for about twelve years. His wife's known him the whole time, so she's probably in on it. This whole thing might have something to do with that. Don't know. The one I owe Dahl is not reporting on Mark Epson's society. The police think making it public will have huge backlash in addition to generating public support. I don't really have any details on the secret society anyway, so to talk about it now would be premature.*
>
> *Long story short: in this folder is the info the police have on this case so far. I had to pretend to be charmed by a Mormon to get it, so it'd better be worth it!*
>
> *Going to sleep now.*
>
> *—K*

Well, bless Kay's heart, she could be useful when she chose

to be. The police report was much more thorough and concise than my trip through Utah Courts and saved me hours of time.

Mark Epson was the head of a college secret society, all right. The police knew this because several of their own ranks had stepped forward as character witnesses. They were former members who swore that their leader was being framed. They risked their careers for such actions, but none of them backed down. They respected Mark and didn't want him in a mental hospital when his little girl was born. To stop that from happening, they were ready to lose their jobs.

Fascinating.

Kay's research also included detailed reports on Epson's many arrests, characterizing him as cooperative after attempting escape. A few times, he just walked up to cops and turned himself in, outlining the crime.

I wanted to meet this guy. Ten bucks said Kay did too.

As if sensing I was reading her handiwork, Kay called me right as things were getting interesting. It was tempting not to answer, but she deserved better.

"What's going on?" I asked in place of a more friendly greeting.

"So I have two guys with me who want me to take an envelope full of cash."

She had my attention. "As we speak?"

"Indeed."

"And you're talking to me?"

She sounded annoyed. "Of course I am. Should I take it?"

This was weird. "What do they want?"

"For me to do my job and reveal Mike Epson's sordid past."

Oliver and Company wanted Mark Epson's life on the news? Why had they bribed me to stay off the case, then? With my involvement, Kay would have had the info I held in my hands without calling in favors with a cop. Putting it on the news would have been a no-brainer for her.

These guys weren't making sense.

"I'm confused," I admitted.

"You're not alone. So? Should I take it?"

"Day two on the job is kind of soon to make the local police your sworn enemies."

"There's that," she agreed.

"Still, you've wanted to run the story since the moment you heard it, right?"

"Right."

"But now that they're telling you to do it, you're annoyed at them for coercing you to do something you wanted to do anyway because it makes you feel like maybe you were wrong to want to do it?"

"Couldn't have said it better," she agreed.

I could relate. "Is the guy talking to you wearing his Clark Kent glasses again?"

"He sure is."

I sighed. "It's up to you, Kay. Do what you think is best for you and your career. Remember, I'm out, so this choice is on you."

"But—"

"Tag," I interrupted. "You're it." It was the best I could do under the circumstances to tip her off that I was back on the case. No one listening would know, though.

"Well, sounds like I wasted a call," she snapped, but I knew it was all for show. "But since all of you can hear me now, let me make it clear that I will tell this story when and how I want to! That said, I'm not exposing the secret life of Mark Epson until I have a firm grasp of who he is and what effect this report will have on the community. I don't care how much money is in the envelope. My career is too important for me to kill it this soon with a bribe scandal, so kiss off."

Then she hung up on me.

And in that moment, something told me things were about to get very interesting.

FOURTEEN

WHEN MY DOORBELL rang twenty minutes later, I knew who pushed the button. I was getting a feel for Oliver and Company. Since they had failed to control Kay, it made sense for them to approach me to do it for them. Their reason for doing so was part of the bargain they had initially struck with me.

No one would get hurt.

Packing up the folder into my bag, I organized my thoughts as I went to the front door. If my two favorite thugs were at the door, it was because they were going to try to escalate the situation by adding something new to the deal. They wanted something more than mine and Kay's cooperation. I wasn't quite sure yet what that was, but unless they were playing some sort of reverse psychology mind game, they wanted Mark Epson exposed for being the ring leader of a secret society. Had Mark hurt someone along the way? Was he competition?

I laughed at my own thoughts. Competition? Yeah, right. But why did Elliott's little clan want this one lone guy gone? And why do it this way? With the missing puzzle pieces I had at the moment, I couldn't come up with a scenario that made sense. But maybe my boys would throw me a bone.

Whipping open the door without checking the peephole, I spotted Oliver and his muscle on the other side.

"That didn't take long," I said.

"Ms. Jensen," he greeted.

"Mr. Westman."

He stiffened. "We need to talk."

"Strange. I thought our business was concluded," I replied, leaning against the door frame. "I've kept my side of the bargain and so far, you have too. That makes us good in my book."

To my surprise, Oliver's sidekick, Muscle Boy, reacted to that, sending Oliver a little signal I'm sure was perfectly understood before being disregarded.

"We appreciate that," Oliver said. "Now we just need your friend to do her job." He kept his face military straight as he spoke, as if inflection and expression had been trained out of him.

"So one reporter said no. Give the story to another one! Someone's bound to bite."

Neither man blinked, although Muscle Boy was a little tenser than he had been when I opened the door. He didn't like something on his radar, but what?

"That's not the plan," Oliver said.

"Plans can change." Really, it shouldn't be that hard. Muscle Boy clearly didn't mind adapting, so what was Oliver's hang-up?

"We don't need to modify anything if Ms. McCoy will do what any reasonable reporter would do."

His words struck me like a slammed door in the face.

I knew what was going on.

I had been in Oliver's shoes before—eyes slightly squinted with stress, sweat along the brown and down the back of the neck. His breaths didn't come at a full, even pace, but were shallow. He was stressed. He was under orders from someone he either feared or wanted to impress, and that person had told him to have Kay break the story. Maybe the boss had even said it flippantly, just because he knew her name from Elliot. It didn't matter. Oliver and Company had their orders, and their competency was on the line.

How many times had Elliott done that to me my first year working with him? Sent me off to accomplish some impossible task as if it were nothing?

One thing was certain: Elliot and I were going to have a talk. Very soon.

It seemed to me that Oliver and Company were simply trying to prove themselves, and Kay's cooperation was one of the details they needed to cross of the list. So was Mark Epson. Apparently I had been the first to roll over and play dead by accepting their envelope of cash, which totally sucked. What all this meant, though, was that their plight against Mark may not be personal at all. Just an assignment to prove their effectiveness.

At least I wasn't confused anymore. Just as I had once been trained, others were now being trained. Only these guys weren't as green as I had been, and the stakes seemed to be much higher. Their endgame meant exposing someone to public outrage and leaving a pregnant wife to deal with whatever backlash came her way.

Had I been hired to expose people's secret lives in the past? Sure. Many times. Women were frequently hired to get men to say and do stupid things. Who knows, if I weren't trying to play "good girl" in Utah, I may have taken on something like the Epson case back home and been in Oliver's shoes. I totally would have taken a different angle, though. Oliver's tactics made no sense.

"Are the wheels turning in your head, Ms. Jensen?" Oliver asked.

I stayed silent and let him watch as they kept turning.

"If your friend doesn't do her job, we'll have to force her." He used his throat muscles to force his larynx down as he spoke in an attempt to be threatening. He was fronting in hopes of intimidating me. The fact that I had taken the envelope so quickly on our first meeting made me the weak link in his book. That would come in handy.

The game had officially changed, but poor Oliver just didn't know it yet. In the new version of the game, I knew the stakes: Oliver's pride. How far would he go to stroke his own pride? How overt was he willing to be?

"And how do you plan on doing that?" I asked.

"I plan on getting her attention." Again, he didn't blink. "Unless you can talk some sense into her."

I never would have made a move like this, even in my rookiest of days. Men like Oliver should execute orders. They just weren't good at thinking on their feet. The whole situation was a mess.

I stepped forward, getting in his face. "I can smell the sweat on you, Oliver. You know why?" He exhaled and paused, not breathing back in and still trying to intimidate me with his eyes. But he waited for me to finish. "Because you're painting yourself into a dangerous corner.

"You have no idea what you're talking about," he sneered. Another mistake on his part. Responding with greater emotion than you're addressed with is a sign of fear and defensiveness. He should have known that.

"Choose a different reporter," I repeated. "No one will care."

He stepped away. "Clearly we're done."

"Clearly."

They turned their backs to me without another word and headed for their pimped-out Escalade.

"Don't forget our deal!" I called after them.

Neither turned. Neither spoke. Neither acknowledged me in any way.

Translation: the deal was off. And if I didn't want to deal with Oliver's rogue tactics, there was only one thing to do. I would have to get him fired.

FIFTEEN

I NEEDED ANDY TO stay under the radar for a while. Some primal voice deep inside warned me that if Oliver and Company reappeared, I might not like what happened next. Kay would be next to impossible to hide, and the first thing she would do if I got her off-grid would be to jump back into the action. Then there was Ty. Crap. What in the world was I supposed to do with him while I played chess with Oliver?

I doubted my new friend would take kindly to me getting him fired. But drawing Oliver's fire felt safer to me than not knowing who or what else he might be aiming at. The last thing I wanted was to be blindsided by a move that would haunt my dreams. I already had enough bad things lurking there to torment me.

Which brought me back to Ty. There was no question he was on their radar. And if I made a move they didn't like, they were going to counter it with a move I didn't like. Someone like Oliver would retaliate to show me how serious he was. Kay fought dirty. She would see a move like that coming. Ty and Andy, though? Things like this didn't exist in their world.

I needed to talk to Kay, but more than that, I needed to think ahead. I needed to tune into that instinct that peeked into the future and knew what waited. I needed to do what

Andy always begged me to do and pray.

The impression I received while doing so was of leaving home with all my counter-surveillance gear in my trunk and my backpack filled with tactical gear. In the pack, I also had my bribe money and a variety of guns. I hate guns.

Marksmanship was important to my job, and I owned an assortment of firearms—tranq, dart, rubber, beanbag, and the real thing—but I hated them. It was nice to have a variety, but I'd promised myself never to use a real gun anywhere but on a firing range. "I'm not taking real bullets," I whispered to no one at all, as if that made everything all better.

Money and guns. Packing those up and heading out into the world didn't exactly paint me as a good guy, but if Oliver was willing to point and shoot, I needed to be willing as well. Yet another reason to stick close to Kay: The woman didn't hesitate when she looked down a barrel, and she was a crack shot. On the off chance I lost my nerve completely, I could just hand the guns to her and promise to pay to have her manicure redone when she grumbled.

But what would I tell Ty? What *could* I tell Ty?

If I thought about that too long, I would be paralyzed into inaction, and every moment I wasted was time I handed to Oliver as a head start. First things first: I needed to pack my bag and head for Kay's while keeping myself bugged. It wasn't time to let them know I knew about their surveillance yet. For now, everything stayed above board. Oliver and Company might even like that I was visiting Kay. They'd assume their tactics worked and that I was there to beg Kay to cooperate. I could work with that.

Taking only my bag with its updated contents, I hopped in my car and headed down to the news station. Kay would be waiting, if only subconsciously. The girl could work under pressure, but something like this would grate on her. Plus, she'd just turned down a thick envelope full of money. She'd be cranky.

The temptation to alert Andy as I covered the short distance to the station was strong, but once I did that, the red flags would go up and there would be no going back. At present, I had a more immediate concern—where to park. On the street, it would be easier to tag or otherwise compromise my car. If I parked in visitor parking, the same things might happen, but then I had only one exit point.

I was way too paranoid.

My phone buzzed with a text. *She's not at the station. You'll find her at Mark Epson's.*

The number was blocked and there was no signature, but it didn't take a brain surgeon to figure out who sent it. Oliver was texting me now? Was it yet another scare tactic? Was I supposed to be freaking out for the camera or something?

Whatever the desired response, Oliver wanted me to talk to Kay, so there was no reason not to work with that. Turning east, I headed up toward the University of Utah to have a little chat with my friend and figure out our next move.

SIXTEEN

I SAW KEN DAHL before Reporter Barbie when I reached the Epsons. What was he doing there? Furthermore, what was Kay doing squaring off with him like they were in a lovers' quarrel?

Curiouser and curiouser.

Uniformed officers surrounded the house, searching for something, which was even more curious. I'd have to ask Kay what that was about. Ignoring a street sign that informed me it was permit parking only, I parked and joined the party. Neither Kay nor Dahl noticed my approach. They both seemed very intent on each other.

"Ms. McCoy, if you know something regarding the investigation, you need to share it." His deep baritone voice claimed an authority from another time period. Give him a drawl and some spurs, and he'd fit the bill for a cowboy outlaw from a western movie.

No wonder Kay was furious. It was either seethe or swoon.

"I don't know anything, Ken." She busied herself with her mic but otherwise held her ground. "Now if you'll excuse me, I have a story to walk through."

She tried to walk away, but he gripped her arm. "Just last

night you were scared out of your mind and hiring a body-guard. Where is he?"

So that's what she had told him to get the report.

"Just out of sight. Waiting," she snapped back. "I really appreciate everything you did, but I overreacted, okay?"

"Uh-uh," he said, pulling her in with enough force to have her eyes narrowing. "You want me to believe you're fine? You want me to think that you weren't using me last night? Where's your bodyguard, huh? Did you even hire one?"

I stepped in before Kay could reply. "Yes. And you'd better let her go before I make you."

Both of them turned to me in complete shock. Luckily for Kay, Officer Dahl was taken so off guard that he didn't catch her biting back a laugh. Yes, my timing rocked. But it was total luck.

Once the surprise wore off, Officer Dahl was indignant. "*That's* your bodyguard? A hundred-pound girl?"

"Absolutely," Kay said without blinking an eye.

"We need to talk," I insisted before Ken Dahl could get any more conversational traction. Kay and I needed to get on the same page.

"No problem," Kay agreed, and I pointed to her news van. She nodded.

"Nice meeting you, Ken," I said as we walked to the van and got in. Before shutting my door, I flipped on my jammer. Oliver and Company wouldn't be listening to this conversation. And with any luck, they would chalk the interference up to the broadcast equipment in the van.

"I love you," Kay said the moment the doors were shut. "That was so beyond perfect. Beautiful, really. If you weren't already my hero, you would be now."

"It was good timing," I agreed. "But we have bigger issues."

"That's an understatement! I was hoping that you had a

plan from what you said on the phone."

"The beginnings of one, yes." I looked away and took a breath. "It would be simpler if Andy and Ty weren't in the picture. I don't know what to do about them, honestly."

She bit her lip, and I knew she was on the same page—at least where it came to Ty. Andy she might throw to the wolves. I wasn't sure.

"So what do you know?" she asked.

"My car has a camera in it and my bracelet is bugged." I held it up for effect and Kay's mouth opened in horror.

"They can hear us right now?"

I shook my head. "I have a jammer on for the moment, so no. Once we make our move, I'll get rid of all their surveillance, but until then I'm letting them have that little sense of control."

"Okay," she nodded, considering. "But what's this whole obsession with Mark Epson? What do they want?"

"Mark might be the best one to answer that question. Did he mention anything?"

Kay shook her head. "Nothing. He and his wife shared a few telling glances, but he didn't say anything."

"Maybe we need to motivate him then," I mused.

She sent me a sidelong look. "You volunteering?"

It had the potential to be tricky. "I guess. But once we disappear, our Mafia guys are going to start making dumb choices. We have to figure out where to stash people. I think I have Andy covered, but I don't know how Ty could disappear without coming with us."

"What about Officer Unfriendly?" Kay said, jerking her thumb toward her new favorite cop. "I could turn on the estrogen again."

That actually got a smile out of me. "For the cause?"

"Yeah, so don't say I never take one for the team."

"Mm-hmm," I replied, mulling over the idea of making

Ty stay with the police. If we could orchestrate it without them asking too many questions, it might be perfect. "Do you think you could get that to happen?"

She tapped her finger on her leg in thought. "Yes, but not now. Right now he's all wired about the anonymous tip."

I looked at the officers searching the premises again and noted one man in particular who stepped out the front door and onto the porch. He wore dark pants and a long-sleeved grey shirt. It was the uniform of a division of law enforcement I luckily didn't see often. "Clark Kent called in a bomb threat?"

Kay nodded. "They'll ask us to leave soon, I'm sure."

Why hadn't they already? "What did the threat say?"

She pursed her lips, looking guilty for the moment. " 'Key personnel know what to do so the Epsons don't lose their home.' "

I looked back at the house. "So not a direct bomb threat."

"But there's a possibility. That's the guy from university security. As soon as the Salt Lake bomb squad gets here, they'll kick us out."

That didn't make sense. "How did I beat them?"

She shrugged. "Does it matter? The point is that we can't sit in here and talk all day. What's next?"

What was next, indeed? I seemed to be avoiding that part. "I've figured out what our boys are about," I confessed. "I'm going to try to shut them down, but I would feel better if you stuck with Ty while it went down." I could have slapped her and she would have been less offended. "I'm serious, Kay. I don't like this Oliver guy. He's too impulsive." I looked her in the eyes, letting her see my concern. "He'll pull a trigger."

She stared right back. "So will I."

I knew that. It's why I hadn't brought bullets. If she got one of those guns in her hands, I didn't want her doing something she would regret.

"Two of them, two of us," she tacked on. "You can't face

them all alone with no one watching your back."

It sucked that she had a point.

I took a stabilizing breath, trying to pinpoint what the sick feeling in the base of my stomach was warning me of. "For now we should probably—"

The impact of the blast hit me like a bat to the chest. Next to me, Kay's shrill scream let me know I hadn't imagined the explosion. And if that hadn't been enough to convince me, a man in uniform hit the van's windshield and shattered it inward.

SEVENTEEN

K EN?" **IT WAS** the first word out of Kay's mouth as she searched for the door handle. On the dash in front of us, the officer groaned. It wasn't Officer Dahl.

"You okay?" I asked the man. He gripped his stomach.

Though the windshield glass had fragmented into cubes, I could still feel where small shards had embedded themselves in my exposed skin. Up my arms and definitely on my face and eyelids, little pieces of glitter stung like a rash. I knew what had happened, but my mind tried to reject it. I looked around in a daze for several seconds while Kay fought to push the passenger door open.

Debris from the home fell around the van and into the street, forcing cars to screech to a stop. I finally dared to look at the house only to see the front and top of it blown off.

Oliver and Company just blew up the Epson home. Was he insane?

In my pocket, my phone buzzed with a message. Given the disastrous circumstances, it made sense to ignore it, but the timing was too eerie. It had to be from Oliver. With shaking hands, I reached for my phone.

Stop trying to be smart. We will not be trifled with.

Trifled with? I hated him in that moment. Kay finally

fought her way out the door, and I remembered that if she was here, so was her cameraman. Had she brought Nick? Was he one of the bodies laid out in front of me?

"Ken!" Kay called. She must have been delirious, or she would have kept the fear out of her voice.

"Where's Nick?" I yelled to her.

"Camera!" she exclaimed as if the whole world suddenly made sense again.

"Kay, where's Nick?"

She turned to me on her way to opening up the back of the van. "Getting a sandwich. He'd better hurry!"

Thank heaven he'd been away from the blast! The officer on the hood groaned again, and I angled to see his name tag. "Officer Caldwell, are you bleeding?"

Sirens drowned out his response as the bomb squad showed up and patrol cars popped out of nowhere. Before I could ask again, a paramedic came to the side of the van and checked Caldwell's pupils.

"Are you okay, ma'am?" he asked, giving me a quick glance. "Can you exit the vehicle?"

"Yes," I said, reaching for the handle. If it didn't work, I could climb out the window.

"Can you walk?"

"Yes."

In less than a minute, the site had been transformed from a semi-urgent search for criminal tampering into a disaster zone. Bodies that had lain still after the blast were starting to move again, trying to get back to their feet, some with debris sticking out of their prone forms. They were the ones who needed the medical attention. I was merely stunned.

"I'm good. Take care of him," I said, nodding toward Caldwell. I needed to find Kay, and if I wasn't mistaken, she was unloading the camera from the back of the van. I got out and ran around to meet her.

"Good," she muttered, handing me the massive thing. "Can you hold this? You remember how it works, right?"

The woman was in shock and dialing her producer. Behind me, Nick ran up at full speed carrying a Subway sack.

"What happened?" he said, staring at what was left of the house.

I held out the camera to him. "It blew up."

He looked at Kay. "Is she . . . ?" Hurt? Okay? Insane? He couldn't seem to pick a word.

"Calling in your exclusive?" I finished for him. "You betcha. Now take the camera and get ready to be bossed around."

"We're going live as soon as the feed's up," she said, slapping her phone shut. "How's my hair?"

"Hopeless," I confessed. "Forget about it and just get the exclusive." The word acted as a trigger, snapping Kay back into full attention and allowing me to fade into the background. I would try to find Ken. It seemed like the right thing to do for reasons I couldn't define.

How close had he been to the house when it blew? I had to be helpful somehow. If I asked anyone in authority, they would tell me to get out of the way, but that wasn't what they needed at the moment. Maybe in five or ten minutes, when they had enough emergency personnel, but the first few minutes after an incident were pivotal.

"Ken?" I called out, just before spotting him tearing the sleeve from his shirt to make a tourniquet. He was fine.

"Rhea?" A familiar voice called from behind me, and I turned to face a man I hadn't seen in weeks.

"Detective Scott?"

He ran to me. "What are you doing here?"

I needed to tell him about Oliver. "Telling you who did this. Got a notepad?"

He didn't hesitate or even ask me if I was delirious, which was flattering under the circumstances. He just reached into his breast pocket for a notepad as I started talking.

"Oliver Westman. At least that's what his ID said. Nevada driver's license. I'm writing the number down," I said, taking both the notebook and a pen from him. "Don't know if it's real or fake. He and another man are traveling together in a new black Escalade with a STRUT grill and Nevada plates." My hand started moving, writing everything I was saying. "I have his number on my phone. He's not blocking it anymore, which means it's an unregistered pay as you go, but maybe you can find out where it was purchased or at least trace the signal."

His eyes regarded me in full cop mode. "How do you know this, Rhea?" I think he tried to keep the accusation out of his voice, but I heard it anyway.

"Westman paid me to stay off this case. He said as long as I stayed away, no one would get hurt." I held up my hand to stop Detective Scott before he started yelling at me. "He texted me and sent me here. This place didn't blow up because I showed up. Westman decided to blow it and then sent me here." Or at least I was pretty sure that was the case. He had called in a threat, after all.

Detective Scott took the notebook back from me and looked over the details. His face was not friendly when he looked at me again. "You should have given this to me sooner."

"I was being watched. Closely."

A muscle jumped in his jaw. "I don't care. You made a bad choice here, Rhea."

He was right. If I'd been smarter, uniformed men might not be scattered on the ground. Still, I needed to point something out for my sake, if not Detective Scott's. "I may have screwed up, but I didn't blow up that house, detective. Now you've got the facts I've got. See if you can find Oliver Westman before I do."

He shook his head. "Stay away, Rhea, or I *will* arrest you."

Arrest? That made me think of protective custody, which made me think of Ty. Closing in on him was the logical next move.

I had to go!

But first, there was no better time to ditch my bug. Pulling off my bracelet, I exposed it for what it was in front of Detective Scott when I yanked off the cover entirely. Usually I pulled what I needed out of individual pockets, but I didn't have time for that.

He stepped closer, focusing one item in particular. "Is that what I think—"

"Yes," I snapped before he could finish. I didn't want to talk about it. I just wanted to find the tracker and—

Something fell and bounced to the ground beneath me. Both Detective Scott and I looked. I didn't recognize it but knew a transmitter with a tiny mic when I saw one.

"That's all yours if it helps," I said as he bent to pick it up.

"You've got to be kidding! It's tiny!"

"But it works. I've got to go make sure someone's okay."

Behind me, I heard Kay starting her broadcast. "This is Kathryn McCoy broadcasting live from the site of an explosion that took place moments ago on Douglas Street, just a short walk from the University of Utah campus."

Acting on pure reflex, I grabbed my phone and quickly texted her all the info I'd just given to the police. After pressing send, I ran to my car, checking to see if she had noticed. I couldn't hear her anymore, but I saw the tension in her shoulders a moment before she glanced at me. I held up my phone and wiggled it until I saw her understand. Then I got in my car, pulled the cover off of the dome light, ripped out the camera, and floored it to Ty's gym.

EIGHTEEN

DON'T KNOW WHAT I expected to find, but it was business as usual at Gold's Gym. Fit bodies strutted at their usual pace, completely unaware of what had happened three miles away. No Escalade was parked in the parking lot, nor was any other high-end car with Nevada plates. I raced in the front door where Tiffany, the usual check-in girl, stood at her post and sent me a big smile.

"Hi, Rhea. Here to see Ty?" she asked, all chipper.

Could everything really be fine? "Yeah. Can you page him please?"

"He's with a customer," she said. "They just started."

Without explanation I pushed past the desk and went looking for him.

"Rhea?" she called after me. I ignored her. If Ty was just starting a session, he might be doing a warm-up, which would put him in the cardio area. I started there and found him in less than thirty seconds. He stood talking to a little twig of a girl on an elliptical. A natural blonde, she looked like a freshman in college at the oldest as she sucked in her stomach, pushed out her chest, and over-laughed at something he said. His body language was noncommittal, but definitely not discouraging. When he saw me, he stepped away from the girl.

"Rhea? What's going on?"

I looked at the girl. "Sorry, he's going to have to reschedule this session. Family emergency."

She blinked in surprise. "Everything okay?"

"No," I said, grabbing his arm and pulling. "I need you to come with me now!"

He didn't budge. "What's going on?"

"Come with me and I'll explain."

He took a few hesitant steps before his eyes dropped to my neck. "Are you bleeding?"

"Maybe?" I offered. "We've got to go."

I didn't have to drag him then. He was all but pushing me as we moved to the exit. "What's going on, Rhea? Why didn't you call?"

"Because my phone's cloned. Yours probably is too. Do have it on you?"

"Yes," he said, fishing it out of his pocket as Tiffany and a scowling manager came into view. The manager looked us over and reassessed the situation.

"Everything okay, Ty?" he asked.

"No," I answered for him. "Emergency. I'm sorry, but I have to steal him. He won't be in to work tomorrow." I snagged his phone as I spoke. After pushing through the door, I popped the back casing from Ty's phone and removed the battery. There were only so many places to hide a tracker, and I didn't see one.

I didn't give the phone back to him. "Stand next to the car," I commanded, and though he looked like he wanted to object, he didn't.

Opening the driver-side door, I pulled out a wand and ran it over him, finding no transmitters. Good. If they were tracking Ty at all, they were probably doing so through his truck.

"Okay, get in."

"Why are you bleeding?" he asked, his eyes still focused on my neck. "What happened?"

I bent into the car to turn on the radio to an all-news station while I made a sweep around the car to make sure it was still clean. It was a smart move, since the thing started beeping when I passed over the right rear bumper. I'd been tagged. Removing it and tossing it away, I finished my scan of the rest of the car.

It was clean. Ty watched all this in silence as he listened to the breaking news. When I moved to get in the car, he did the same, noticing immediately that the dome light was exposed.

"You were there?" he asked, indicating the story on the radio.

"Yes. And I need to make you disappear so you don't become a target."

He blinked in surprise, not seeing how he had anything to do with me witnessing a house explode. I couldn't blame him. It dawned on him soon enough.

"Wait, is this about the whole thing with Elliott and how he's not in the Mafia? I thought you decided to stay out of it!"

I whipped out of my parking spot. "In the end, it didn't matter."

Now that Ty was safe with me, I had three more things to do before I went off-grid as well. Item Number One: Elliott. I had to dial him using my number, or else he wouldn't pick up. I wasn't sure he would pick up anyway, but he did on the third ring.

"Hey, beautiful," he cooed. "How's the desert?"

"We're not friends right now," I said, turning east to a tactical position.

"Back up, my dear. What's going on?"

I fought the urge to weave through traffic as Ty listened intently at my side. "Your men crossed the line."

"*My* men?" he echoed, incredulous. "In Utah? I don't think so."

"They're wearing your ring!" I accused.

He didn't respond.

"What, no comment?" I said

"Rhea . . . I can't." He sounded nervous. "Are you sure it was the same?"

"Positive."

He swore under his breath. "Then we can't be talking. I can't tell you anything. It's how it is. Do you understand?"

"No," I snapped, although there was a chance that maybe I did. "They said if I backed off, nothing bad would happen, but they just blew up a house, Elliott. Cops—many cops—were injured. I'm dealing with power-hungry idiots here."

The lights were timed so that I pushed straight through them without even touching the brakes. I didn't have much time.

"Does that sound like someone I trained?" Elliott asked, his voice cautious, as if he knew the call was recorded.

He had a point. "No. But then how did they know I worked for you? It's one of the first things they said to me."

"Good question." A question he clearly wasn't going to answer.

I wanted to punch my steering wheel, scream, anything! "You promise, Elliott? You have no idea what's going on?"

"None. Think about it, and you'll realize my sphere of influence. No poaching or interference is allowed. I'm sorry. If I cross the line, I open the door for others to infringe. It's the rules."

He was giving me clues. I didn't understand them yet, but I could sense it in his tone.

"This is all bigger than me, Rhea. Good luck." He hung up on me. I kept my phone at my ear for a moment, stunned, as the road curved right and turned into Parley's Way.

Confused or not, it was time for Item Number Two: Andy. I did so without a word to Ty, although I could see him watching me choose the number in my phone book.

"Hi, Rhea!" he said when he picked up, his voice all bubbles and light.

"Hi, Andy. I need you to listen, okay? What I'm about to tell you is important."

"Uh, okay." He sounded like he was waiting for a punch-line to a joke.

"I need you to disappear. I need you to take the cell phone battery out of your phone and go somewhere no one could ever find you. I'm dead serious, Andy. Taking Marissa with you wouldn't be a bad idea."

Silence.

"Remember those guys who were waiting for me with the tricked-out Escalade yesterday? They just blew up a house, and I have no idea why. They saw you that morning, and I don't want them finding you right now, so I need you to disappear. Do you understand? Park your car at a hotel and disappear."

"You're serious," he breathed.

"Completely. I'm sorry, Andy. I have no idea how this happened or what's going on."

"But I have to do this? You're sure?"

"Unfortunately, yes. I wish I wasn't. Do you understand that this is serious?"

He let out a deep breath, clearly thinking. "Yeah, I do."

Good. That was good. "Just another story to tell the kiddies," I said, trying to find a rainbow.

Looking ahead, I realized I was running out of road. I needed to end the conversation with Andy.

"I warned you the first time we met," I joked. "I told you my life was a little crazy and that I wouldn't make a good Mormon."

"You're not a bad Mormon," he said, but his heart wasn't in it. Like any person would be doing, he was thinking of his next move.

"We'll debate that later. Promise me you'll disappear?" I

begged. "You have to promise me so I can concentrate on what I have to do, Andy. Disable your phone, ditch the car somewhere safe, and disappear. I need to know that you can do that."

"I can do that." He didn't sound excited about it, but who would? "I'm kind of hoping this is a joke. When will I know it's safe?"

Good question. "I will personally leave a message of your sister's favorite scripture on Marissa's phone. Then you'll know."

"You have Marissa's number?" he asked, confused.

"I'll get it. Now go. Take out your battery the second we hang up and get to business. Sorry again,"

"Good luck, Rhea." He hung up.

Ty shook his head. "Thank you for not giving me a call like that," he said, his voice hushed. "I would absolutely freak out."

What could I say to that? Nothing. So I just sent him a sad smile. We'd reached the staging point for Item Number Three: Kay.

Pulling to the side of the road, I opened my phone. *Ditch your phone. It's cloned. No more contact. Stick with Dahl. Maybe buy a ticket and take a holiday under an alias. Love you!* The moment my phone showed the message sent, I flipped it over and removed the battery, just like I had with Ty's.

"You're freaking me out, Rhea," Ty said softly.

"Yeah? Good," I said, pulling out my SIM card, followed by Ty's. Reaching back for my backpack, I pulled out a zipper pack that held eight back-up SIM cards. I installed them and stuck the battery back in Ty's phone. When it rebooted, I entered the new SIM password and made sure the GPS tracking was off, checked the number, and handed him the phone.

"They can't track you now," I said, doing the same with my own. Once it was set up, I gave his new number a call so my phone's number popped up on his caller ID. "Save that number. This way we can stay in contact."

Putting the car back into drive, I headed up the street, trying to focus on the bright side. If there was an ideal spot to fall off the radar, this was a good candidate. The road ahead of me forked into two diverging freeways, one eastbound, the other southbound. Yet another road split north, back into Salt Lake City, and if I flipped a U-turn, I would be headed back the way I came. Oliver would have no way to guess where I'd gone, especially after the text I'd sent to Kay. If they were already tailing me, I'd spot them down the road.

"We couldn't be in a worse car," I muttered to myself and then shot Ty an apologetic look. "I need a second to think, okay? I'm about to take the long way somewhere, but when we get there, I'll explain everything."

Face pale and not at all thrilled, Ty nodded and turned up the radio to listen to the news.

NINETEEN

USING RESIDENTIAL STREETS to avoid traffic cameras, it took me nearly thirty minutes to get to an indie laptop store. Getting out, I grabbed Oliver's envelope from out of my backpack and took a small stack of 100s.

"Do I have to wait out here?" Ty asked, looking miserable.

If Oliver and Company found us, there was no way I wanted Ty separated from me. "No. Come on in."

His tension lessened as we exited the car and headed in the double doors. My eyes quickly scanned the merchandise on the front display as a salesman approached me.

"That one," I said, pointing to a 15-inch MacBookPro with a dual processor. "I'll give you three thousand dollars right now if you hand me one I can walk out with in under two minutes. You keep the change."

Greg, the wiry salesman, looked at me like I was joking, so I tapped my wrist where a watch might be. "Tick-tock, my friend."

"She's serious," Ty said quietly, as if he was worried we'd be overheard.

"Two minutes," I repeated, making sure there was no smile in my eyes.

Greg faltered. "But we need to register—"

"I swear I'll come back and do that later, but I need it right now. Yes or no?" I held up the bills so he could see them.

"Yes! It's a deal!" he said and ran to the back. I counted out the cash for his return.

"Just had that lying around?" The accusation in Ty's voice hurt, but how could I blame him for wondering why I had a wad of cash? I couldn't.

"It's the bribe money to stay off the case. They broke their end of the deal, so all bets are off. I'll explain when we're safe."

He looked around, incredulous. "We're not now?"

I pointed to my car. "As long as that car is visible from the street and we're near it, no." To my relief, that made sense to him, so I continued. "If I were actively taking cases, I would have a minivan or last year's bestselling SUV. We'd be safer if there were twenty thousand Audi R8s in the Salt Lake Valley, but there aren't. It's pretty much just me, which means every time we pass a traffic camera, anyone watching for us knows for certain they've got the right car. Tracking a Honda or a Toyota would be a much bigger nightmare for them."

"These guys can do that?" he asked.

I nodded. "If I can do it, I have to assume they can do it. After all, they just led me and Kay to a house and blew it up. I'm not putting much above them."

Greg was taking longer than I liked. It had nearly been a minute, according the wall clock.

"None of this seems to faze you. You did stuff like this in L.A.?" Ty asked.

I hesitated. "Sometimes, but this is the first time I've been forced into someone else's game."

Greg emerged with a box. "All ready to roll! I threw in some extras as well." He looked so proud of himself.

I took the box and handed him the money. "Thanks,"

I said, heading for the door while he counted. Ty was right behind me. He didn't say another word, which was both the best and worst thing he could have done.

TWENTY

USING A FAKE ID, I checked us into the airport Holiday Inn. It was lucky that Ty and I were both runners because I parked at the airport four miles away and we ran over to the hotel. Being the gentleman Ty is, he carried my new computer while I hefted the backpack. I wasn't ready for him to know what it held yet.

Once we were behind closed doors, Ty positioned the only chair in the room to where I was setting up the new computer on the bed.

"I don't understand how this all happened," Ty said quietly.

"Me neither," I agreed. "But it's got to end quickly, and that means showing the shot caller what idiots these guys are. If Elliott sent me on a case like this and people traced it back to him, he would have dealt with me without hesitation." I cringed at the mere thought. "It would not have been pretty."

"So that's what you're going to do? Try to track down his boss?"

I nodded, attaching the power cord to the computer. "That's why I needed the computer—one they can't trace, especially when they don't know where I am. I could have driven to Arizona, for all they know. If they find my car at the airport, they'll spend a good amount of time trying to find where I flew to. They're frozen for the next bit, unless they're psychic."

He took a steadying breath. "So what can I do?"

Our eyes met, time stilled, and suddenly I had to touch him. Crossing the room, I stood in front of him to look down on his upturned face. "Don't die and don't hate me. I think that's pretty much all I can ask from you."

"Done and done," he said, pulling me down into a kiss. Man, I needed that. It was a nice call-back to reality. I wasn't used to a guy having my back when it came to insane situations. I definitely wasn't used to being kissed in the middle of them.

But, as always, he pulled away before it got too interesting.

His smile was slow and brilliant. "Get that computer up and running so we can end this, will ya?"

"Yes, sir," I agreed, and moved back to the bed, realizing I needed a few other tools.

"Can you get me a notebook and multi-colored pens?" I asked Ty, fishing out a hundred-dollar bill for him. "Cash only. If they don't have change, just buy other stuff until you hit a hundred. Be casual. Don't draw attention. Just be a tourist."

He nodded, taking the money. "I think I can do that."

"Thank you. I should be ready for them by the time you get back."

"Just focus on that," he said, heading for the door. "I'll be right back."

He was right. I needed to get the computer up and running, but I kept thinking about Kay. Did she understand the message I sent her? And Andy. Did he make it off grid? And all those officers? Had anyone died? As of the last radio report, no one had. Total miracle.

Okay. Time to the bottom of all this. Oliver Westman needed to be shut down. Fast. I had my starting point: Elliott.

I'd never looked into him before, but wherever there was organized crime, there was a legitimate-looking paper trail. Money
needed to trade hands, and it needed to do so without raising
any flags.

Follow the money. It was Elliott's mantra, and I was now
using it against him. *Sorry, boss.*

Technically, Elliott had trained me for situations just like
this. My entire first year as a rookie investigator had comprised
of getting myself out of tight spots. I could do this.

Internet up, I dove in, creating parallel profiles for Elliott
and Oliver until I hit a brick wall. Knowing what I had to
do next, I looked up to the ceiling and said, "Sorry if this is
against holy rules or something, but I gotta do it," before dialing a number I hadn't used in over a year.

"Mario's Pizza. We don't deliver," a familiar voice said.

"Dingo," I replied. "It's a clean line. I'm looking for bank
records."

On the other side of the line, Dingo chuckled. "Is this who
I think it is, Ms. Jensen?"

"The very same," I said, not in the mood to chat him up.
Dingo lived a secluded life, either hacking software or develop-
ing it, and part of his payment for services rendered seemed to
be giving him someone to talk to.

"I thought you didn't like me anymore," he flirted. "You
disappeared."

"I just ran out of cases worthy of you, but I've got one
now—if you're up for it." Had to challenge the pride of men
like Dingo.

"Up for it?" He let out a guffaw. "Please. Challenge me. It's
been awhile."

"You know Elliott?" I asked.

"Church? The guy who introduced us?" he clarified.

"The very same," I agreed. "We're doing him."

On the other side of the line, I heard his hands clap

together. "Ha! Honey, I've had his accounts flagged for years. I've always liked watching his activities. Never boring."

Very handy. "Good, because we're going to cross reference him with someone."

"Oh, that's even more fun," he said, fingers clicking away on his keyboard. "Almost there."

"I'm good with time," I said and let it go silent. I had no small talk for him.

"So you're back in the biz?" he asked, pushing the conversation for me. "I'd heard you joined a cult and started building Jaycos."

Okay, the guy could be funny. "Not quite," I laughed. "I have been out of the game for a few months, though. The guy's name I'm about to give you forced me back in."

"Yeah? How'd he do that?"

No need to beat around the bush. "He blew up a house and injured about a dozen cops."

Dingo gave a low whistle. "And he's connected to our Elliott?"

"Let's call them distant cousins," I said. "Although, I'm hoping not too distant or we won't see a digital relationship."

"Gotcha," Dingo said. "Elliott is up. Who's your second guy?"

"Oliver Westman. I've got all his basic info but the social."

"Is the name an alias?"

"Possibly," I admitted. "Although he introduced himself as Sam, so I'm hoping the ID he had on him at the time was real."

"Let's pull a photo and find out. If you want to see what I'm seeing, I need you to visit my site and download the software. I'm not seeing you right now."

I hesitated. "You burn my position with anyone and we're through, Dingo. I've got to make that very clear. I've got collateral with me."

"Rhea, Rhea, Rhea," he sighed. "It hurts that you even feel you need to clarify."

It wasn't an answer. "I'm clarifying because I don't know who you choose to answer to. Are we clear?"

"Crystal and pristine, my love. Now let's get synced."

I knew where to go and what to click without him telling me. "I wish you had a nicer site to download from, Dingo. You've got to work something out for your female customers."

He laughed at me. "Men of power have one thing in common, Rhea. This site has a 98 percent success rate in finding my audience. Deal with it."

I did, just like he knew I would. And even though no box popped up asking me to okay the software download as the video cued, it was all part of the design. I wouldn't doubt it if Dingo had hacked a million different computers with this same site, without anyone knowing it. I was just glad Ty wasn't in the room.

"Gotcha," he said a few seconds later, and I closed out of the video. "Okay, I'll start putting all this on your screen."

The bank records appeared—the offshore ones first—and a soft whistle escaped me before I could stop it.

"I know, right?" Dingo said. "Your ex-boss is not a boring man. Oh, and it looks like Oliver Westman is your thug's legit name. How'd you get it?"

"Picked his pocket," I said, trying to grasp what I was looking at.

"Well, good on you. At a superficial glance, they don't have much in common, but they do share banks and timing of automatic deposits, so I'd guess you're right about them being part of the same parent organization. I'm going to throw up some side-by-sides for you."

"Thank you."

I heard him catch his breath before he uttered something I really didn't want to hear. "Whoops."

"Whoops, what?" I asked.

"I just hit a trip wire. We need to disengage while I do damage control. Anything you close out you lose, got that?" On the other side of the phone his fingers flew across his keyboard.

"Got it."

He hung up.

Well, this just kept getting better and better. I wasn't sure what Dingo meant by "trip wire," but I wished him the best. In the meantime, he'd managed to get the nitty-gritty on Oliver Westman in front of me, including the bank records of accounts not linked to his debit card.

For the record, his occupation was listed as "private security," and his employer was a security firm in Vegas. All legit, all above board, despite the large sums of money changing hands. The sums didn't concern me for the moment, though. All I wanted to know was who was transferring the funds and where they were getting their money.

Ten minutes into looking, Ty returned to the room with a bulging shopping sack from a neighboring hotel.

"They didn't have multi-colored pens at the gift shop," he explained, unloading what he'd scored. Toothbrushes, toothpaste, deodorant, a dozen protein bars, and probably twenty bottles of water accompanied the notepads and pens. All of this would come in handy.

"That's fine," I said, not wanting look away from the screen as I searched for the umbrella corporation directing the flow of funds to Elliott and Oliver alike.

"The sales girl did talk me into matching T-shirts for us, though," Ty said, sticking his hand back into the bag for something else. "She says they're all the rage." He pulled a brown shirt from the bag and tossed it across the bed to me. Bookmarking my place on the screen, I caught it and took a glance. In large, bold letters it declared, "I CAN'T . . . I'M MORMON." It was my size, and I couldn't keep my nose from wrinkling.

"And you got one too?"

He nodded, smiling. "It's funny and I need to get out of my gym shirt. Apparently these guys know where I work."

"Yes, well, it's a good thing this one is much less obvious." If he heard my sarcasm, he ignored it. I gave the shirt a sniff and tossed it across the bed. "It smells like new shirt."

"That's bad?" he asked. "I thought new smelled good."

"New car, maybe," I said, turning back to the screen. "New shirt, no way. Can I steal those pens and notebooks?"

"Yeah," he said, reaching into the bag and coming to sit next to me. "What are we looking at?"

"Numbers," I replied, leaning back so he could see more easily.

"Whoa! You're not kidding. They're like twenty digits."

"Pretty close," I agreed.

For a moment we just looked at the screen together.

"I hate to ask," he said. "But, but would this be easier to sort in Excel?"

I nodded. "For sorting, yes, but you really don't see a lot of this info unless you physically write it. I remember things better after I've written them. On the screen they can jumble, and I'll forget."

"Oh." There was a beat of silence. "Yeah, I can see how that would happen."

We shared a smile, but Ty grew somber in the middle of it. "Kathryn's not broadcasting anymore. They still have someone broadcasting live, but I think they sent Kathryn to the hospital or something."

I nodded. "She's smart. She'll be safe."

He rubbed his thumbs together, clearly worrying. "I wish I felt as confident."

"You'll see," I said gently. "The girl's a cat."

"I'm sure you're right." The words came out of his mouth

with no faith, and his worry settled heavy on me. I couldn't have a hovering worry-wart, so I grabbed the remote.

"Want to order a movie or something? I'm going to be boring for a while."

He shook his head. "No. I'm good." He pulled out a second notebook he'd apparently bought for himself. "I got my own stuff to figure out."

Stuff? As in "us" stuff? Financial stuff? What stuff?

I didn't ask. "That's good." And we both went to work.

TWENTY-ONE

TY AND I both jumped at the harsh knock on the door two hours later. After a shared look, I popped up and moved to the peephole. I breathed a sigh of relief and let Kay in.

"You could have told me you were checked in under *my* alias," she griped, wearing her approximation of gym clothes as she walked in. Then she saw Ty and relaxed. "You got him."

"Of course I did," I said, noting her apparel. She looked ready for anything. "Were you tailed?"

She shook her head. "Nope. Went shopping on the way home, took off everything, put on the new stuff, and left everything home. Cell phone, the whole deal. I won't even tell you how I got here. That's a saga saved for the day we're able to laugh about this."

Ty stood and hugged her. "Glad you're okay," he said.

"Ditto."

He inhaled deeply by her neck and sent me a smile. "You smell like new shirt."

"Ugh. Tell me about it," she groaned. "Point is, I'm clean. And I would have been up here twenty minutes ago if Rhea would have used one of her own aliases."

"The text specifically said *you* should take a holiday," I said without apology. "I didn't say *I* was taking one."

She grunted, not liking that I had a point.

"Wait, you both have aliases?" Ty cut in. "Who are you two?"

Kay rolled her eyes as if the question wasn't worth her time and faced me. "How far are you?"

"Looking for the tip of the umbrella through digital trails."

"Which means you're leaving one," she reminded me.

I pointed to the new laptop. "Yes, but at least I'm starting with a clean slate. I haven't done anything that would attract attention yet. I'll save that for the end if I have to."

Ty raised his hand. "Is this normal jargon for everyone but me?"

Kay sent him a smile, noting the new shirt from the gift store that he'd put on. "Wow, Ty. Really? You want to advertise that?"

"What?" he looked down. "It's funny."

"If you're sixteen," she corrected.

"Yeah?" he reached for the second shirt. "Well, I got one for you too."

She caught it with no effort when he tossed it her way, and to my surprise she actually seemed amused by it.

"I would tell Rhea to wear this," she said. "But it would have to say 'I'm *trying* to be Mormon.' "

"I'm doing pretty good!" I said, walking to my backpack to grab her a phone.

"Rhea, if they gave grades in religion, you'd get a C, tops. I know, because once you hit a B or an A, we may not be able to hang out anymore."

I held up one hand to hush her while handing her a gas station cell phone with the other. "If there was ever a time not to talk about all that, it's now."

"Just sayin'," Kay drawled, sounding smug. "But back to the point—I'm clean but I do have bad news of a sort."

Bad news? "Do I need to know it?"

She bit her lip and nodded. "You'll want to know this, I think."

I folded my arms and waited while she scrunched her nose.

"Wow, now I have to figure out how to say it," she hedged. "I thought it would roll off my tongue easier since I hate the guy."

"Andy?" I gasped. "You know something about Andy?"

Ty stepped forward, eyes worried. "He was supposed to disappear."

A Cheshire-like grin filled Kay's face. "He approached the police as a 'concerned citizen' and told detectives he thought you might be involved in the bombing. He offered his services in helping the police track you down, should they be required."

Ty's hands flew to his mouth as an involuntary laugh escaped him. His eyes were wide with a disbelief that I shared.

Kay continued. "Your friend Detective Scott pulled me aside at the scene and told me all about it. And don't worry, I told them Andy had a target on his back, and if they let him walk back out onto the street, it might become a problem. He's taking care of it."

"Wow," Ty breathed. "What was he thinking?"

"That our Rhea is a criminal," Kay said with artificial pep.

I shook my head, trying to refocus. "He clearly thought he was doing what was best."

"Sweetie, he turned you in!" Kay reminded me.

"I got that part," I said, turning away. "Ty, get the number off that phone and call Kay so she has your new number."

"That's it?" she asked. "No rants of disbelief?"

"I have to focus." And I did. Flipping out would have to wait until later—probably when Andy and I came face to face again. I knew that I had flexible morals with a comfort zone that expanded outside the norm, but I'd never imagined Andy to be such a straight arrow. A tattletale—even when he didn't have the facts!

If I didn't stop thinking about it, I might pop. Andy had completely disregarded the warning I'd taken a huge risk to give him and served himself up on a gold platter for Oliver. If Andy got hurt, it would be his own fault, but I would forever feel guilty. It would take about that long to forgive Andy for his complete idiocy and lack of faith in me.

Ty rested his hand on my shoulder. "Try to see it from his point of view," he coached softly.

I stepped away so he wasn't touching me. "I can't. Not right now. I need to finish this."

It was hard to miss Kay's smirk as I moved back to the computer, but I ignored that too. Petty politics like the games she and Andy were playing didn't mean a thing at the moment.

"How's *your* boyfriend?" I asked to distract her.

Ty wiggled his eyebrows and turned to her. "Boyfriend?"

"Yeah, Kay's in love with a Boy Scout cop," I said, leaving her to Ty's scrutiny. It was best for all of us if they were distracted while I dealt with the dirty details.

But two minutes later, Kay was back at my side. "Why are you looking for the boss? We could help the police find Oliver. Why not go after him?"

"He's gone," I said, pointing to the screen, where it showed his bank account had already been emptied. "He's burned and he knows it, and if I go at him directly, it'll all just escalate." I gave her a tired look. "If I wanted you off a news story, coming after you is the wrong approach. Getting you fired from the station with a black eye in the industry is much more effective. That's what needs to happen with Oliver. It's time to turn the money faucet off."

She blinked, her mind syncing up with mine. "What can I do?"

I pointed to her new phone. "Keep your ear to the ground for news. Something might blow this thing wide open. Only call grunts and landlines without caller ID."

"On it," she said, and whipped open her phone.

TWENTY-TWO

MONEY. THE MORE you accumulate, the more complicated managing it becomes. Usually those in the middle and lower classes are taught to work for money so they can spend it. Affluent people don't believe in spending—they believe in investing. They want money to work for them, not the other way around. If someone hands them a dollar, they don't go looking for something that costs a dollar, and they don't stick it in savings. They look around to find a way to turn that dollar into five, and those five into twenty.

The ways to do this are mostly limited by the imagination of the investor. But in order to take Oliver Westman down and send him back to Sin City, I needed to pinpoint the responsible holding company.

When a parent company or firm owns enough of another company's stock to basically control latter's board of trustees, the former is referred to as a holding company. Basically, those with deep pockets can invest in a promising business without providing any goods or services. All it does is fund the business through the purchase of stocks.

Seeing the actual holdings of a single company can be eye opening, especially if you've ever stopped to wonder who owns a corporation like Coca-Cola.

Well, Coca-Cola owns Coca-Cola, right?

Are you sure? What about Nike? Proctor and Gamble? Tesco? Conoco? Wells Fargo? Walmart? Who owns them? We're not taught to think about that. Trillions upon quadrillions of dollars move through entities we see more as icons and scenery to the same few holding companies owned by the same few men.

Elliott's company was in someone else's holding. At least, it had been at some point, and I needed to find out who put stock in Elliott's success. Then I needed to find who owned Elliot's backers, and so forth until I had an actual person's name. But I needed more than bank numbers populating a screen to go down that road, and since I didn't know if I was going to get Dingo back, I had to try to think like him.

Searching both my memory and the Internet, I kept one ear open to Kay while she called her press release room and grabbed updates. Ty sat on the next bed over with his new notebook, writing furiously. Despite everything, I wanted to know what was in that notebook.

But I had to focus.

Finding the first link was fairly easy, but I was looking for people, not companies. It's one thing to say S. C. Johnson & Company owns Windex, but that still doesn't give me names of actual people. And even if it did, it doesn't tell me who made the push to acquire Windex.

I glanced at my phone, wanting to call Dingo back, even though I knew it would be idiotic to do so. Going through all this data by myself would take me days.

Dingo could do it in an hour.

Kay covered the mouthpiece of her phone with her hand as she continued to listen to someone on the other side. "Stay strong," she whispered. Clearly my discouragement was obvious. Kay made a few more grunts of acknowledgment before piping up again. "Thanks, Neil. This is perfect." Then she hung up.

"Good news?" I asked, open to distraction.

"The Escalade was found abandoned in Sugarhouse, and it's been taken to processing. No sign of Oliver or his henchman. They're both underground."

Not necessarily good news in my book. I preferred to imagine my target was hiding from me and possibly regrouping. Someone like Oliver wasn't the type to go hide and lick his wounds. I'd handed his principle ID to the cops and he knew it. That put me near the top of his hit list, as far as I was concerned.

"Any casualties from the explosion?" I asked.

She shook her head. "Doesn't sound like there will be. Everyone's stable right now—a few have even checked out."

A sigh of relief escaped me. "That's good."

"The police are all over it, obviously," she said, sitting at the foot of the bed.

Ty looked up from his notebook, tension obvious on his face. "But they haven't found anything yet, right?"

"They will," Kay snapped.

Kay? Defending the police? This was a new development. Liking a "Ken Dahl" was one thing. Putting faith into his ability to do his job was another thing entirely. This was obviously a conversation for another time, but whoa! I needed to know what the two of them had been talking about while I'd been laying low.

Just then, a chat box popped up on my screen.

>>Who'd you piss off? I think they knew you were coming.

Dare I hope that it was Dingo?

>>*Mario?*

>>Of course. Got a present for you. You're about to be flooded.

>>*Bless you!*

>>I take cash and wire transfers.

>>*Send me the bill.*

>>Will do. And if you're open to opinions, looks like you're sniffing down The Fours.

>>*Who are The Fours? Do they all wear matching rings?*

>>Yes.

>>*With an X on the face?*

>>Yes. Like the one your old boss wears. I'll save you the time of looking them up, though. No conspiracy theorists have tripped over them yet. Won't find anything online.

>>*Of course not. That would be too easy. Thanks for the heads up!*

>>Sure. No charge for that.

I laughed.

>>*You're a gem.*

"What's funny?" Ty asked, turning to face me at full attention.

For the first time in hours, an authentic smile crossed my face. "I've got my inside guy back online, and he's got good intel." At least, it sounded like he did.

>>Here it comes.

Windows started popping up faster than I could count them. While they were still appearing, Dingo wrote one last comment.

>>Going dark again. They're trying to trace my trail. If they get me, they get you. I'm out.

The chat window closed just as the last of the windows populated my screen. "You might have consolidated them for me," I grumbled. I clicked through a few windows and realized that he had.

Holy crap. This was going to take time.

"Anything helpful?" Ty asked as Kay dropped on the bed next to me. She swore when she looked at the screen.

"I was going to offer to help, but nevermind. That might as well be Chinese in my world."

"Yeah," I breathed. In my world it might be a step above Chinese. Maybe Latin. Some of it I could guess at, but all in all, it would be best if I just became a quick study. Thank heavens for Google.

Kay handed me my notebook the moment I reached for it. "I'll stick to keeping my ear to the ground," she said.

"Thanks," I agreed. "We want to know the temperature of things when we walk out that door."

Face grim, she nodded.

"And may I take this moment to mention how bad it sucks not to have some secret skill," Ty said, eyeing us from his bed.

I could have comforted him—told him it was all right and not to worry about it—but that would only unman him further.

"Note taken," I said instead.

"Even if this never happens again, I want some secret super skill I can pull out of a hat."

"Gymnastics," I said without thinking. "That comes in handy more than you might think."

Kay nodded. "Definitely. And don't feel bad, Ty. My superpower is the ability to broadcast into people's homes. Nothing too special, really. But we'll find you a Scooby skill to go with your new decoder ring."

He smiled. So did I. It felt good to have a normal conversation for ten seconds.

Everything would turn out all right. It had to.

TWENTY-THREE

BY FIVE O'CLOCK, the natives were restless, and I was just barely sketching out a picture of what we were dealing with. When a call to the front desk revealed that the hotel rented out gaming systems, Ty and Kay officially stopped griping and the wagering began. They were killing each other on Halo as the sun disappeared behind the horizon and the September sky filled with stars. Not that I was looking at them, but they called to me.

Nighttime would be the best time to make a move. The dark provided good cover, and with a car like mine, I needed all the help I could get. Renting a car had crossed my mind several times, but I didn't want an unfamiliar and possibly unreliable car taking me on a treacherous business trip. Conspicuous as it was, my car was the best option.

I watched Kay, her hands subconsciously jerking to correspond with her shots fired on the screen. She looked so young when she was with Ty—like the girl in her twenties that she was, not a cutthroat newswoman or a missionary-hater. It did me good to see her relax and act like the person I knew her to be when we first met.

It meant the world to me that Kay approved of Ty and let her guard down around him. She'd never been like this around Ben even, and those two had history. Whatever magic Ty had, he worked it on both of us . . . luckily in different ways. His chemistry with Kay was very, very platonic, while ours was, well, not.

"You did *not* just hit me with a fire bomb!" Ty roared.

"Sure did," Kay said sweetly. "Deal with it."

Kay would insist on coming with me. She might be decompressing now, but once I made a move, she'd be on me like a shadow. From a morale standpoint, it felt great to know I had willing backup. From a responsibility standpoint, it scared me to death. The chances of something happening to her were high, if only for the simple fact that it was extremely likely that something would happen to me as well.

I brought my focus back to the contents of my screen, though my eyes weren't focusing so well anymore, which was another reason to have the notebook. It gave me a break from staring at a screen.

A picture was indeed coming together, but it had absolutely nothing to do with Mark Epson. Mark was a homegrown Utahn with no secret accounts and no national affiliation. He supported local businesses and a "green" lifestyle. His arrest record might be longer than the usual citizen's, but all of his crimes exhibited a playful quality to them. I hadn't met the guy or his pregnant wife, but I couldn't see any action on his side that merited his being targeted to the degree he was.

"Hit pause," I said, looking up. "I need a powwow."

Kay hit pause before I even finished the sentence and plopped down Indian-style on the bed, while Ty pulled the chair out from the desk area and sat on it.

"What's up?" Kay asked.

"Mark Epson," I said, putting my computer to the side. "How does he fit into this mess? Why target him at all?"

"And," Kay added pointedly, "is it coincidence that they did so on my first day reporting here? That question's been bugging me."

I nodded. "It's a valid point, since obviously we've both been on their radar from the beginning."

"Does that make you targets?" Ty asked.

Kay and I looked at each other, neither knowing the answer.

"Which brings us back to Mark Epson," I said. "Neither Kay nor I have a connection with him, and I feel pretty safe in saying that we never would have met him or heard his name if all this hadn't happened."

"Agreed," said Kay. "He seems to be the king of his very small pond and happy to stay that way. After interviewing the neighbors today, they all seem to know the Epsons and think they're nice, but I didn't get the sense that they were any more than acquaintances. They're nice, but they keep their distance."

They sounded like me. I knew my reasons for staying an arm's length away. What were the Epsons' reasons? And how organized was their little pond?

"I want to talk to them," I muttered, wondering if it was possible. They had to hold the key to all of this, or Mark wouldn't have been chosen as a fall guy.

"The Epsons?" Kay clarified. I nodded.

"They must be in a hotel or something, right?" Ty asked.

"With police protection," Kay said.

That bummed me out until I remembered that I wasn't in L.A. I didn't hate the police in Utah. I actually had a few friends on the force. "Anyone we know watching them?"

Kay shook her head. "I didn't recognize any of them, but I only know a few names."

"Where's Dahl?" I asked.

"He was taken to the hospital and released, but he's banged up enough that they have him on leave for the next forty-eight hours."

Neither Kay or I was saying it, but it was a miracle that

both of us had walked away with nothing more than a pepper-
ing of glass slivers. If Kay and I had been standing outside the
news van, instead of sitting inside it, we would both be in the
hospital right now. And if the presence of all those cops hadn't
forced me to park a ways down the street, my car might have
gotten a lot more than a shower of sheetrock.

All in all, we'd been totally blessed.

"Could we still call him?" Ty asked. "I mean, assuming
he's not totally doped up on painkillers?"

Kay's eyebrow furrowed. "Ken doesn't strike me as the
painkiller type. He's more of the 'pain is weakness leaving the
body' type."

"Which means he'll be annoyed that he's been sidelined
just as things are starting to get interesting," I said.

"Probably," Kay agreed.

We all considered that a moment.

"Is it really important that we know why they chose Mark
Epson?" Ty asked after a moment. "Is it a need-to-know item
or a want-to-know?"

For a moment I didn't answer, mostly because I'd never
really seen Ty as a critical thinker. He was my go-to guy for
fun and carefree adventures. We were breaking into whole new
territory here with him providing serious feedback in a case.

And he was good at it.

"Required? No, but knowledge is power. It's best to know
what your opponent knows, or you can fall into simple traps."

"Like what?" he asked.

To my surprise it was Kay who answered, and her response
was something I would have never expected. "Like people not
knowing that I hate being called anything but Kathryn."

Ty processed that and looked between us. "Except Rhea.
She can call you whatever she wants."

Kay nodded carefully. "And why is that, Ty?"

A heaviness entered the room that silenced his initial

response. I waited while he reconsidered. "She can call you other names because she knows which ones bother you and why."

I stared at Kay. Was she seriously considering letting Ty in on that part of her life? One look in her eyes told me that, yes, she wanted to. The same look told me, however, that she wasn't going to do it until all this was over.

"Regardless, you never know when what you don't know will bite you in the butt," she said instead. "We have fewer bargaining chips if we don't know how the Epsons fit in."

"All I can think is that maybe one of Mark's stunts went wrong at some point, and someone close to Westman was affected," I mused.

"Or maybe he refused an offer," Ty chimed in.

Kay laughed. "That's so Hollywood."

"Doesn't mean it's not true," I said. "I wish we could get a list of members of his little secret society and cross check them with Westman's associates."

"Which would be a huge waste of time if Westman is just following orders from someone higher."

I thought about that. "No, he's too reactionary to be unconnected," I decided. "We go radio-silent for five minutes, and he blows up a house? That feels like he's invested personally to me."

"It does," Ty agreed. "Not that I'm an expert, or anything, but it sounds like he's a control freak."

Yes, it did. So who was he more interested in controlling? Mark, me, or Kay? It felt a little narcissistic, but it seemed like Mark was a patsy and that Kay and I were the real targets here. After all, Ty was right—it was only after we went off grid that he blew up the house that he'd sent us both to. Scare tactics.

"I'll agree with that," Kay said, absently scratching her arm and flinching when she grazed some glass. Two seconds later, she had squeezed the offending shard out of her arm and walked it to the trash can. "Will Detective Scott share anything with you?"

"No," I said, slouching against the headboard. "He threatened to arrest me if I didn't leave the case to them."

"Please," Kay groaned. "Scott won't catch a guy like Westman unless he makes a huge mistake."

"Which, arguably, Westman has," Ty pointed out. "Maybe we should leave it to the cops to catch him."

Kay rolled her eyes. "In what decade? The guy cleaned out his accounts, which means he has a back-up plan. City cops don't have jurisdiction over interstate cases, and the FBI would only leverage him to catch someone bigger. In the meantime, none of us feels safe going to work, and we're left to wonder if the next time we turn the key in the ignition we'll be blown to high heaven by a car bomb." She resumed her place on the bed. "I'm with Rhea on this one. We track him while the trail's hot and end this."

"Now who sounds all Hollywood?" Ty joked, but neither Kay or I laughed, causing him to tense. "How far are you two willing to take this?"

Kay shrugged, her posture and voice defensive. "Wherever it leads, as usual—and please spare us the token male posturing about how it's too dangerous or something. It won't change anything."

"Whoa, a little quick with the claws there, wouldn't you say?" Ty shot back. "If you ask me, I think I'm taking all this quite well, considering my girlfriend stormed into my work a few hours ago and dragged me out, telling everyone I wouldn't be in tomorrow. Most guys wouldn't roll with that too well."

"You're a rare gem among men," Kay said, her voice flat and laden with sarcasm. "Which reminds me, Rhea, I'm on trauma leave. No work for me tomorrow either. I'm not going anywhere."

"Thanks," I said. I'd hoped that was the case, but it was good to know for sure.

Kay tapped the computer. "Where are you with all this? Anything coming together?"

"Yes . . . ish," I said, turning the screen to face me for no reason in particular. "I think I have it down to eight, which makes sense. These guys call themselves 'The Fours,' and they seem to operate in pods of four. As best I can tell, mentors choose an apprentice from a pool of pledges and groom him. Ten years later, the apprentice does the same and the cycle repeats, each new generation feeding into the older generations. After that forty-year spread, all of The Fours get to retire around sixty, when they're supported by the four under them with sizable donations until they die. They can still invest and actively earn after they retire, but they're no longer required to pay dues to The Fours ahead of them, from what I can tell."

"Sweet set-up," Kay said. "Kind of brilliant."

"How do they find apprentices?" Ty asked.

"Through fraternities," I said. "They all pledge to the same fraternity."

We all perked to attention at the same time.

"Fraternity?" Kay asked.

"And isn't Mark the leader of a secret society?" Ty finished for her.

Kay shifted to her knees, excited. "What if Mark stole one of their pledges without knowing that he'd been groomed for The Fours?"

"Makes total sense!" Ty agreed. "The pledge refused them, thinking Mark's group is more his style, so The Fours decide to shut Mark down and reclaim their recruit."

I looked between the two of them and could have kissed them both. "Best powwow ever," I said instead and offered up some fist bumps.

"It feels right," Ty said, looking more than a little excited to have stumbled upon a great answer to an impossible question.

"Hundred bucks says it is," Kay agreed. "So now you're just trying to find which of two trails leads to Westman? You said you have eight names."

"Yep, but they're actually the heads of eight trails that all share the same investments as Oliver."

"But that's better than a few hours ago," she said and I heartily agreed.

"Thank goodness for Dingo."

"Dingo?" Ty asked.

I tapped the computer. "My hacker connection. Without him, I'd still be Googling publicly held stocks."

"I'd toast the guy if either of you two drank," Kay muttered, and Ty actually laughed.

"Yeah, because to start drinking would be a great idea right about now, right?"

She rolled her eyes. "How long do you need to narrow it down?"

She asked it as if should be as easy as something routine, like unloading the dishwasher. "Still a few hours. I'd get some sleep if I were you. Let's plan on moving in the morning. We'll probably fly. Five of these eight guys live close to major airports. I can book us a flight, and we can take the hotel shuttle to the airport in the morning."

Kay tensed. "Won't that flag us? Will they catch that? Even if we use their cash, won't they track the serial numbers? I don't have an alias ID on me. I left all that behind."

I hadn't thought of that. "We'll deal with that if it becomes an issue. Until then, feel free to rest up."

"What about you?" Ty asked, looking like he would have reached out to touch me if he were sitting closer. "You need rest too."

"Couldn't if I wanted to," I said, shaking my head. "I'm in this until I have some answers and a plan of action. Might as well have you guys rested up for when I crash."

He nodded, still not looking like he was too happy about sleeping while I worked. "When do you expect we'll fly out?"

Kay's eyes narrowed, waiting for my answer. Was I going to let Ty come?

"It'll just be me and Kay, Ty," I said softly.

He shot out of his seat. "What? Why?"

I drilled my eyes into him. "Because I can't watch out for the both of you, and you have no idea what you're walking into. Kay does. Plus, these guys targeted both of us, which means she should be there when everything is resolved. This directly affects her and her career. None of those things are true for you. You're not involved, except through association, so there's no reason to involve you further."

"Not true!" he argued.

"*All* true," I snapped back. "Ty, if you come, you'll be a liability, regardless of your intentions. I'm not being overprotective—it's simply how it is. Three's a crowd once we walk out of this hotel room."

"And you choose Kay?" he snapped.

This was not going to be pretty. "*I'm* not choosing her, Ty. Oliver did. He didn't call you to make sure you were in the blast radius of a bomb, did he?" He flinched, and I continued before he could say anything. "If Kay wasn't forced into this, I'd be going on my own."

Jaw clenched, shoulders squared, and looking every bit the tousled hero with his five o'clock shadow, Ty squared off against me. "If you think that I'm going to let you—"

"Being my boyfriend does not give you the moral obligation to face off against dragons you're not trained to deal with, Ty," I said over him. "You're in my world now, okay? This is my baggage. I'm not divorced. I don't have kids or psycho exes. I don't have a history of drugs or alcohol or sordid tales of abuse. My baggage is that I chose a career path with high stakes and huge pay-offs. It took a lot of bumps, bruises, and hard lessons to get where I am, so trust me when I say, with the best of intentions, that you're in over your head here, and I'm not going to risk involving you!"

The muscles in his cheek were twitching, and I could see his pulse pounding in his neck. He was angrier with me than he'd ever been. I couldn't care about that or what it might mean for our future. I just needed him to get the message.

"You're not coming, Ty," I said with finality. "I need you to stay right here where I know you're safe."

No one moved for two long, horribly intense seconds.

"I need to take a walk," Ty said, storming out of the room. Kay and I watched him go in silence, not speaking until the door closed behind him.

"He knows not to leave the hotel, right?" Kay asked.

My heart pounded in my head, tempting a headache. Every instinct I possessed screamed at me to chase after him, but doing so would undermine everything I'd just said.

"Maybe you should follow him and make sure he doesn't rent another room under his name or something like that," I told Kay.

"Got it," she said, already off the bed and moving to the door. "I'll take care of Ty. You just get to the bottom of all this."

"Sounds good," I said, even though it didn't. I was the one who should be taking care of Ty, and the fact that I wasn't felt very, very wrong to me.

But all that would have to be dealt with later.

TWENTY-FOUR

DONALD SMITH: SIXTY-ONE, divorced with three children—two girls, one boy—all grown. He had purchased his estate in Teton Village, Wyoming, in the late eighties for $440,000, without financing, apparently. The original lot had been nearly three and a half acres, but he had acquired six additional acres around his home property in the past few years, and over 10,000 acres around the country.

The man liked owning land and, with any luck, that would be my in.

I researched the surrounding plots of land and found that they were all owned by the same company. One of the larger plots had a small stream running through it. If there was a plot Donald Smith wanted to buy next, that would be it. Rural mind-sets understood the value of a natural water source, and Donald had lived a life extracting value from everything. He would want that stream.

I'd found my man, and my "in" to approach him, but kept the good news to myself for the moment.

Spread across the comforter at my feet, Kay had finally succumbed to sleep. So had Ty on the next bed over. He maintained a stony silence when he reentered the room with Kay. He just laid down with his back to me and hadn't moved since.

It was probably just as well.

On my screen, I had the number for Donald Smith's answering service. The trouble was that it was two in the morning. No legitimate business person would call at this time at night. I'd get a live person if I called, but how would I get them to believe that I was doing business in the middle of the night?

Slipping into the hallway, I dialed the number and pressed send. A woman answered on the second ring.

"Mr. Smith's answering service. May I take a message?"

"Oh, I'm so sorry, I just noticed the time!" I apologized. "I'm in Hawaii and didn't think of the time difference."

"Not a problem, ma'am. May I take your message?"

"Yes," I said. "I am a real estate agent representing one of the properties adjacent to Donald Smith's ranch home, and since the property is coming up for sale, I thought I would give him first bid on it. I'm about to board the red-eye to Salt Lake City and will be taking a chartered plane into your area to meet with a few clients tomorrow evening. I was hoping Mr. Smith would like to meet with me regarding the two-point-eight acre strip on the west side of his property."

"One moment," her professional voice said. "Please hold."

Hold? Why was she putting me on hold? Was she actually going to wake Donald at two in the morning? Before my imagination could freak out too much, she was back on the line.

"He would be happy to have you drop by his home at your convenience between the hours of five and seven this evening. He will be leaving at seven for a private function. May I have your name?"

Alarms went off in my head, signaling that all this was happening too easily, too quickly, but I was too tired to look a gift horse in the mouth.

"Sophia Johnson," I said, choosing the name of the realtor I'd bought my house through back in Glendale. "And I will try to get there sooner rather than later."

"Very good. I'll let him know. Have a nice flight"

"Thank you," I said, and we hung up.

And that was it. Piece of cake. I had an appointment with a billionaire that may or may not end up being the most important meeting of my life. The adrenaline in my system told me to hit the road right then, but the rational part of my brain warned me that I'd been awake for an impossibly stressful twenty-two hours and had plenty more stress coming at me. I needed rest.

Sneaking back into the room, I closed my laptop and turned off the lights. Four hours. While I would have loved to hit the road before the sun came up, I would regret only giving myself three hours' sleep. Then again, if Oliver had scouts looking for me, I'd be the only car on the road. Six o'clock would be better for blending in. Maybe.

It didn't matter. Tactical or not, I needed at least four hours of sleep if I didn't want to be one cylinder short the next day, so I set the alarm on my phone, curled up, and checked out.

TWENTY-FIVE

MY PHONE VIBRATED, rudely indicating my time for sleeping was over. Though my body was used to another hour, my reason for waking perked it right up. I reached over and shook Kay, waiting for her eyes to focus on me before saying, "It's time."

She got up without a word, moving to the bathroom and shutting the door. I sniffed my underarm, wishing I had clothes to change into and briefly considered Ty's purchase the day before.

No way. Deodorant would have to do.

Joining Kay in the bathroom, we brushed our teeth and got as ready as we were going to get in relative silence.

Ty didn't budge when we moved out of the bathroom and started packing up. His breathing stayed even, as if he was asleep. I wasn't sure, though, since he wasn't a snorer.

With everything loaded up in my pack, I nodded to Kay, who reached over and picked up the bag of goodies that Ty had purchased the day before. I shook my head, indicating she should leave it. She rolled her eyes. Reaching in, she pulled out two protein bars and two waters.

"He has room service," she mouthed to me. "He'll be fine."

She had a point, so I nodded and pointed to the door before turning to Ty. I had to say good-bye.

Moving to stand over him, I squatted down so I could speak directly into his ear.

"I love you," I whispered, saying the words for the first time. He didn't budge. "I hate leaving you, but it really is for the best. If you hate me for it, I'll understand. You're really too good for me anyway." I straightened a little and bent to kiss his temple while tears unexpectedly flooded into my eyes. I blinked them back before one could drip onto him. "When this is over, if you don't hate me, I'm going to kiss the socks off of you, and you're just going to have to deal with it."

A tear slipped out before I could stop it, landing on his neck. I froze, waiting for his breathing to change, but it didn't. The steady rhythm continued. He hadn't felt a thing.

"Be safe," I said at last. I walked quickly to the door, turned off the bathroom light, and shut the door with a soft click.

"He'll be okay," Kay assured me.

"Yeah," I said, not wanting to talk about it. She caught my drift.

"Where we heading?"

"To the airport to pick up my car. We've got a long drive ahead of us, and I think we're going to take the long way."

She grimaced. "Why?"

"Because there will be more cars and cities and less mountain driving."

"Uh-huh. I'll pretend that answer makes total sense," she said, switching the bag mostly filled with water over her shoulder. "Meanwhile, I need coffee."

"We can grab something while we wait for the shuttle."

She grunted, eyes glazed and clearly wanting to go right back to sleep.

"Or you could just sleep in the car," I offered. "We're only driving."

"No dice," she yawned. "I got more sleep than you did. I'm good. I just need my coffee. I'll be my usual perky self in no time."

I chuckled.

"What's so funny?"

"Nothing," I said, still laughing. "Let's get you powered up and hit the road."

TWENTY-SIX

WHEN I POPPED the trunk to stash our stuff, Kay let out a little snort at the spread laid out in my trunk. She had downed most of a double-shot cappuccino and was in much better spirits.

"Someone's prepared for anything," she said as I found a nook for my laptop and took out a scanning wand. "What's that?"

I turned it on and started around the car. "Just making sure they didn't tag the car since I parked it. It'll pick up anything that can broadcast or detonate."

She shook her head, opening the passenger side door and tucking her bag behind her seat. "You are truly paranoid. No way they found this."

The chances of her being right were almost certain, but it didn't matter. In games like this, nothing could be left to chance.

After making the rounds and finding the car clean, I tossed the wand back into the trunk and brought the backpack with me up to the front. I didn't want the contents of the bag more than arm's length from me.

"Did everyone use the bathroom before we left?" I said, putting on my belt.

Kay held up her cup. "Are you kidding? After this I'll need a pit stop in the next hour. Do I get to know where we're heading yet?"

"Teton Village," I said, starting the car and backing out.

Kay eyed the clock on my dash. "So we're looking at ten hours to make a five hour drive?"

I headed for the exit, checking my rearview mirror. "We're leaving time for traffic."

Kay laughed. "It's so weird. Yesterday feels like a dream, which makes all of this surreal, you know?"

I sent her a smile that didn't reach my eyes. "Well, let's hope it stays that way. Maybe we'll just drive straight there, grab some lunch, and then play tourist until my meeting with Mr. Smith."

"Smith?" she echoed. "Wow, that doesn't sound shady at all. Is that his real name?"

"Born and raised," I promised, pulling up to the airport parking cashier and handing her cash. She let us right through.

"So we're using the morning commute traffic as a cover to get out of the city and staying on the busier route because it has a higher speed limit and better roads?"

"You *were* listening before," I said, heading to the freeway.

"Indeed." She held up her paper cup as if offering a toast. "To an uneventful trip!"

"Amen to that," I breathed. An uneasy silence followed that filled the car with a hint of anxiety.

Kay chose to be proactive about changing the mood. "So do I get to pick the tunes?"

"Pick away," I said. The more content and in control Kay felt, the better she would be to work with if anything went down. As it was, I was still praying nothing would. Predictably, she tuned into a country station. I groaned. "No wonder you and Ty get along."

"It's the only real music," she said, her voice holding a little twang.

"Then you're going to like Utah even more. They've got way more country stations than Los Angeles."

She actually smiled about that. "I know."

I bit my lip, wondering if I should bring up what came to mind. Why not? "There are plenty of stables here too. You could bring Lady if you wanted to."

The idea had clearly occurred to her. "When would I ride her?"

"We'd find time," I said, purposefully including myself. "She could easily be kept within a half-hour drive, so you could go anytime you had a few hours and wanted to clear your head."

"You?" she scoffed, focusing in on the "we" portion of my offer. "On a horse? Since when?"

I shrugged. "I'm sure I can pick it up."

"No doubt," she muttered, considering the idea.

We were at freeway speeds heading east to connect with I-15. "You gave up a lot when you moved to L.A., Kay. I'm just saying that you can have some of it back now, if you want."

Her hand picked absently at her new exercise pants, search-ing for a loose thread that wasn't there. "Noted. Now let's not talk about it."

"Fine," I agreed. I'd said my piece, my friend was dis-tracted, and we were on our way to see a man who would either make or break me. I had a few hours of driving to rethink my strategy and Kay's role in it. Maybe her presence would give me more leverage and credibility. After all, I had secured an appointment with Donald Smith but had done so under false pretenses. He had no idea I was coming to discuss The Fours. If he knew that in advance, my car might conveniently end up in a ravine en route. It still might, but that wasn't something I planned on thinking about much.

I took the exit for I-15 northbound while Tim McGraw pumped from my speakers. Not exactly the best thinking music for me as I checked my rearview mirror and noted a Ford F150 accelerating out of an on-ramp. It wasn't speeding, per se, but when it pulled in three cars behind me it settled down.

"I trust you," Kay said from out of the blue. "No matter what happens today, I know I'm safer with you than anywhere else in the world."

If she really believed that, she was being naïve. "Thanks," I said as I checked on the Ford and took another sweeping glance around. The chances of this being an uneventful drive were decreasing by the minute.

TWENTY-SEVEN

WE WERE IN The-Middle-of-Nowhere, Idaho, pulling off the freeway for gas over an hour later, when Kay finally asked, "So, do we have a tail?"

I nodded, fighting the urge not to glance toward the freeway we'd just exited. "Four of them, one of which just got off with us."

She straightened in alarm. "What? The whole time?"

I nodded again. "They've been driving in a box formation around us, two in front, two in back. They rotate positions, but it's been the same four cars so far."

She didn't like that news at all. "How are we going to get rid of them? We don't want them following us the whole way, do we?"

I'd been trying to work that out in my mind and had a vague sketch of a plan. "Not for very much longer, but I'll need your help losing them."

She looked in the passenger mirror. "Which one is it?"

"The white F150. The other three should pull off ahead and wait for his cue to pick us up down the road. Traffic's thinning out, and if they get us alone, without witnesses, they'll make their move."

Her eyes narrowed on the reflection of the F150 in the

mirror. "Okay, so what do I do?"

I turned right into the gas station but kept my motor running. "The two front cars—I'll point them out when we get back on the freeway—have a purpose. It's their job to corral us. Essentially, the rear cars don't want us behind them, and the front cars don't want us ahead of them. We, in turn, want all of them behind us."

"That makes sense."

"Once they decide to make their move, they'll get reckless," I continued. "Maybe they'll just swerve, or one of the guys in the back will start tailgating. The point is for one car to distract us while another one gets into position. You understand?"

"I think so," she said, starting to turn the direction of the truck.

"Don't look," I snapped.

"Right," she agreed, looking at her empty coffee cup instead. "So, if a car starts tailgating us, it's to make us concentrate on what's going on behind us while something else happens in front of us?"

"Exactly, and vice-versa. That's when I'll need you. I'm sure these guys have no problem causing an accident in order to stop us from getting away. I'm going to need eyes looking in front and back, so you're going to be my eyes in the back, okay?"

"No problem," she said, a smile coming from nowhere. She gave my arm a little pat. "See? Aren't you glad you brought me now?"

I didn't answer that and turned off the engine. "Go get something to eat if you want."

"Bathroom and coffee," she moaned.

Her words mocked my already heavy eyelids. "Get me some V-8, will you?"

"Got it."

I watched as the man driving the F150 gassed up. I'm sure he needed this stop as much as I did. Too bad his gas wasn't going to do him any good. By the end of the day, I'd have him cursing his truck and wanting to trade it in for something with torque.

A small gust of wind came through the station, drawing my attention to the horizon. Dark but harmless-looking clouds veiled the autumn sky as the cloaked sun climbed higher. Roads were dry for now, and that's what mattered. If I waited too long, though, I might be dealing with slick roads. That wouldn't end well for anyone. Looking north, I found what I was looking for: a stretch of road that wasn't flat and maybe even a little curvy, where I would try to lose my tails.

Closing my eyes, I tried to envision a scenario in which everyone walked away unscathed. I could only control myself, however, and not the four other drivers. So I prayed that they would drive as defensively as I was going to. If there was an accident, I wasn't going to stop. I had to make that decision beforehand so I wouldn't hesitate later. Protecting Kay and getting to Mr. Smith had to be my only concerns if we were going to make it to tomorrow.

The handle of the gas pump released, indicating my tank was full. I replaced the nozzle and managed a second sweep of my car, checking again for trackers, as Kay came out with our drinks. We didn't talk. We just got in the car and started off toward the hilly stretch of road. It took less than a mile for us to be boxed in again. All my players were on the field, which meant no surprise attacks.

"Okay, everyone's in position," I said, pointing ahead and to our left. "Three cars up on the left. The Buick. You see it?"

Kay leaned forward to see better. "Way up there? The black one?"

"Yes."

"Who'd have thought?"

"That's the point," I agreed. "And I'm sure I don't have to point out the F150 right in front of us."

"Yeah, got that one."

"Good. Those two cars, or whichever ones take the front position, are my concern. Yours will be the two in the back."

"Is that white Mazda one of them? It's been with us ever since we got on the freeway."

I nodded, trying not to show how nervous the RX7 made me. No one bought tires like it was sporting unless they had real business under the hood. "And that's the car I'm most worried about. It's modified to accelerate, so I expect we'll see some more of him when we get down to it. The last one is that silver Impala. It's two cars behind us where the truck used to be. That one might be a problem if it's a fully equipped police car."

"Yeah, sirens would be bad," she agreed. "So what are we waiting for?"

"For civilization to disappear."

She looked around, confused. "Is a Chevron considered civilization in Idaho?"

Leave it to Kay to find humor in an intense situation. As I laughed, I felt some tension leak from me.

"See," she teased, eyes trained on the rearview mirror. "Admit it! You're glad you brought me."

Once again, I didn't answer. This was far from over, and there would be plenty of opportunities to regret my decision in the near future.

"Okay," I said. "Looks like they're going to stay in place. Once we start up this first rise, we're going to make our move."

She turned to look out the back. "Looks good. The Impala's getting behind us."

I switched to the left lane. "Good. Keep talking. You're my eyes back there. Even if I don't answer, I'm listening."

It was time to tease my truck, which was only about twenty

feet ahead of me on the right. I downshifted, plowing past him before he had the time to react, and I saw the Buick respond a quarter mile ahead.

"Both rear cars have sped up," Kay said. "The Mazda's gaining behind you."

Let's see what you've got, I thought as my Audi easily went from 65 to 125. I switched to the right lane and was just about to pass the Buick when it cut in front of me. I tried to switch over to the lane it had vacated, but I moved too soon and it started swerving in front of me, forcing me to slow down unless I wanted to take body damage.

"Uh, Rhea, there's a ravine to our right. This might not be the best spot to play games."

Which is exactly why we are, I thought. If these guys feared plunging off a ravine, they might not be so aggressive.

"Eyes behind you," was all I said, and she immediately refocused.

"Okay, I don't see any other cars, but our friends are all gaining. The Impala and truck on the left, the Mazda behind us. Wait, here comes the Mazda. Speed up!"

Easier said than done. The Buick driver was doing his job in slowing me down. We were now only going 85, thanks to his weaving skills. I jerked the wheel left, accelerated, and succeeded in pulling up next to him. He was quick in his attempt to slam me into the mountain, and I had no choice but to slam on my brakes. He weaved back in front of me as my tires screeched.

"The Mazda's not slowing!" Kay all but screamed. "It's going to hit—"

Taking her flinch as a cue, I jerked right, moving back to the right lane just in time to see the Mazda zip past and join the Impala to square me in again and crowd me back over into the left lane as he paced me.

Crap. Now I had two cars in front of me, one ready to run me off the road, and—

"The truck's behind you now and moving up fast."

The Mazda in front of me was slowing, and in just a couple of seconds, I would be trapped against the mountain.

Downshifting again, I shot through the hole between the Impala and the Mazda, just as the road started up again, and kept gunning the engine, even when the Mazda swerved to smash me into the rail. What happened next was what you get when you buy an Audi instead of a Mazda. Kay screamed as we shot forward with a force that slammed her head against her headrest. The Mazda missed my rear bumper by inches and settled for pulling in behind me. Now I just had to deal with that stupid Buick, which was now straddling the lines between the two-lane highway. All pretense was gone now, and traffic laws no longer applied.

I zigzagged between lanes, making it impossible to pull up next to me without crashing, but couldn't build speed because of the Buick. He was slowing on the hill too, and if I didn't take advantage of that, then I would end up boxed in again. It was now or never.

Pulling into a tailgating position, I saw the Buick driver check his rearview mirror.

"Talk to me, Kay."

"The Mazda is about thirty feet behind you and closing. The other two are right behind it. Everyone else is staying away."

The Buick driver's head snapped back a split second before his break lights turned on, but it was all the warning I needed. I tapped my brakes, jerked left, and slammed on the gas.

The surprise and fury I saw on the driver's face as his window passed Kay's was no doubt the cause for the stupid move he made next. Possibly forgetting for a moment that he had front wheel drive instead of rear, he jerked his steering wheel to ram us with his foot still on the brake, and nearly flipped. The fact that he didn't spoke well of his training. He pressed on the gas again and got control of his bouncing rear tires before they caused him to roll.

The mistake forced his friends back, however, since they couldn't pass until his car was under control, and by then I was in sixth gear, going 100 . . . 120 . . . 150 . . . 180 and then slowly inching up to 200.

Kay chanted expletives next to me as she gripped the door handle and held on while I was praying that a deer wouldn't decide to cross the road right then, since it would probably cut us in half before I even saw it.

I don't know how many women appreciate the scream an Audi R8 makes when performing at the top of its limits. Most women are probably too busy screaming themselves, like Kay was, but for me it was a spiritual experience. And with no other cars in sight, I prayed some stupid cop wasn't out on a speeding witch-hunt. I needed to gain as much ground on these guys as I could now that I had them behind me, and I was too busy trying to keep my nose straight in the crosswinds and timing breathers for my engine to concentrate on much else. My whole goal was to get so far out of reach that my four tails would have little choice but to give up.

I couldn't count on that, though.

For five minutes, I kept the car above 180, which meant I was at least seven miles ahead of my four friends. I slowed to 150 then, just to be a little safer and, after five minutes of that slowed to 120, which was a speed that would allow me to respond to radar before I was under the gun. It was only when we were at that relatively low speed that Kay spoke to me.

"I don't know if it's sweat or urine, but my seat is wet."

I gave her knee a little pat. "I don't smell anything. Are you okay otherwise?"

"Besides being mentally scarred and being cured for any future need of coffee in my life? Fine."

"Good."

She turned around and looked out the back window as she had done when we first started. "I don't see them."

I checked the rearview mirror, already knowing I would see nothing but empty road behind us. "We were covering three miles a minute for a while there. Hopefully there's about ten miles of road between us now and we won't have to worry about seeing any of them again."

"Ten miles?" she breathed.

"You were fantastic, by the way," I praised her. "I don't think I could have done that without you."

She shook her head and sat back in her chair. "I'm just going to breathe for a while, if you don't mind."

"Breathe away," I said, and eased up to 140 again since I saw forest ahead and no cop between me and it. Once the trees grew thicker, I would have to slow for safety reasons, so it was best to cover as much ground as possible until then.

I was slowing down to 70 when Kay decided to do more than breathe.

"Have you ever gone that fast before?"

"Not on a freeway."

She slowly let out a breath of air. "That is easily the most freaked out I've ever been in my life."

I smiled. "Is that why you were screaming?"

"Heck yeah!" She paused and beamed at me. "Notice I said 'heck.'"

"Noted. Proud of you, girl, on more than one count."

She took another look back. "Do you think we're done with all that now? Do you think anyone else will come looking for us?"

Her timing was ironic, because right then, with me going exactly the speed limit, a police cruiser zoomed around a bend in the road, lights flashing, and passed us. My eyes locked with the officer's right before he passed, and I knew he wasn't passing on accident.

Pressing down on the gas, I sped for the next exit.

"Did you see that cop?" Kay asked. "It's lucky we weren't speeding just then."

"He was looking for us," I said, pulling off the freeway.

She looked back with intrigue, but then her face turned doubtful. "Are you sure, Rhea? I don't see him anymore."

"I guess we'll find out, won't we?" We were still in the middle of nowhere, and as far as all I could tell, my turn-off led to a group of trees. It would have to do.

Pulling into the trees, I turned the engine off and reached for my backpack. "You want to be the decoy or the shooter?"

Kay grinned. "Do you even need to ask? What kind of gun?"

I picked a gun and handed it to her. "You get tranqs. I don't want this guy radioing in."

"*If* he's a bad guy, and *if* he's following us," she clarified.

"Of course," I said, checking my watch. "If he doesn't show in five, we'll hop back on the road."

"Fine," she agreed, opening her door. "In the meantime, I'll go conceal myself and stretch my legs in the woods. What's the magic word?"

"Handcuff," I decided.

"Done," she said and started away.

"Don't go too far," I called after her. It was unnecessary to do so, but being as paranoid as I was at the time, it made me feel better.

If she heard me, she didn't respond, and I decided to stretch my legs as well.

Getting out, I shut my door behind me and reached down to touch my toes. My muscles complained, but that was to be expected after the stress I had just put them through. Above me, birds gave hesitant and sporadic chirps between the gusts of wind that made their perches sway. I looked up just in time to see a white puddle of turd drop from the sky and hit the top of my car with an accusative thump.

"Not used to having guests?" I asked the chirpy sky. "Don't worry. We won't stick around too long."

The sky was suddenly silent, and I decided to search my car for something disposable to wipe the mess up with.

I was bent over, head in my car and rear out, when I heard the crunch of tires on dirt. We were no longer alone. How had the officer found us so fast?

Making the motion casual, I ducked out of the car and watched the patrol car pull up. When I had pulled into my little nook, I had taken into account the fact that the officer would have a camera mounted on his front dashboard. More than anything I did not want to appear on that camera, so I had purposefully parked so that the officer would have to park perpendicular to me. It gave him the added advantage of blocking me into the spot, but that was something that could be negotiated later.

As predicted, he pulled behind me so that our cars formed a capital T shape. I was off camera and hopefully Kay would be too.

Taking his time, the officer appeared to gather a few items in his car. He didn't touch the camera, though, and that was all I cared about. Neither of us wanted this documented.

He stepped out of the car, leaving the door open behind him and taking a few steps in my direction. "Running from the law, ma'am?"

I gave him an amused look. "Just stretching my legs, officer."

He didn't blink. "In a grove of trees?"

"I thought I'd get off the road," I said with a shrug.

"Well, you certainly did that. Can I see your license and registration, please?"

I didn't move. "For what?"

He took another step forward. "Are you going to make this difficult, ma'am?"

SHERALYN PRATT

"I'd just like to know why you're asking. Are you going to give me a ticket for parking in the trees? If so, that's not a moving violation and you don't need my license."

He did not look happy. "Look, young lady, don't make this hard, okay? You're a long way from home and—" His voice cut off as if he had just remembered something. "Where's your friend?"

I furrowed my eyebrows in confusion. "What friend?"

By the set of his jaw, I knew play time was over. That was too bad, because Officer Bingham, as his badge identified him, was too cute to be a bad guy—and too young. He sported a crew cut, and his chocolate eyes would have been quite attractive under different circumstances. He was a guy that used his looks on the ladies, you could tell. The crow's feet around his eyes told me that he wasn't shy with his smiles.

"You know who I'm talking about," he snapped. "Blonde hair, blue eyes. I saw her in the car with you."

I raised an eyebrow. "And you got her eye color from that?"

He took another step forward. "Let's not make this hard, Rhea. As a rule, I like to maintain the idea that chivalry is alive and well, so if you'd just get in the cruiser with me, someone has some questions they'd like to ask you."

I chose not to call him out on knowing my name. He was getting too close, so I decided it was time to throw out a test. "Just me? What about my friend?"

He hesitated, his eyes dropping down and to the right as he held his breath and clenched his jaw. It was the tiniest moment, but it happened in slow motion in my mind, and I knew the next words out his mouth would be a lie. "She can go free if you want. I was just told to bring you in. I promise that if you come with me, your friend will go free."

Free, but he'd made no reference to Kay being safe. I

held my hands out in front of me. "Are you going to handcuff me?"

His mouth opened to respond, and he leaned forward to take a step just as a dart stabbed him in the neck. He looked confused for a moment, then angry, then unconscious as his legs collapsed under him and he fell forward, hitting the ground face first.

"Man, this thing packs a punch!" Kay exclaimed, coming out from behind a bush. "What's in these darts?"

"Let's just say it's black market." I moved to the unconscious Bingham. Kay joined me.

"I didn't know someone could be knocked out that fast." She reached out to touch him as she said this, and I snatched her hand away.

"Let's get some gloves on," I advised.

She hesitated. "Okay, that sounds spooky, Rhea. What exactly are we going to do with him?"

"Get both him and his car out of our way so we can get out of here. Don't walk in front of his car, either. He has a dash camera."

"Gotcha."

Together we stood and headed back to my car where I handed her a pair of latex gloves out of a box. Her calm manner as she put them on was unexpected, and I decided to comment on our situation.

"Nice shot."

"Thanks. I nearly shot him on reflex when he asked about me. Why did you wait so long to cue me?"

"I wanted to find something out."

"If they were after me?"

I nodded.

"I know. I was so relieved when he said he'd let me go. I mean, that means we were overreacting, right? Why would they let me go if they wanted me dead?"

I was glad she had interpreted Bingham's comment that way. I had no intention of informing her that I'd come to the opposite conclusion.

Gloves on snug, I reached for two other items and turned to Kay. "We'll move him first. Together we should be able to drag him out of the path of the car and push his car out of the way."

"Okay," Kay agreed, breathing easy until we stood next to the guy. "Are you sure he's going to be okay?"

"One hundred percent," I encouraged, plucking the dart from his neck. No need to leave evidence. "Now grab his hand."

After a few good tugs, we had moved him well out of the way. Kay leaned over him. "He's cute."

I smiled, leaving her and walking to his car. "Maybe you two can go out after all this is over."

"Ha ha," she mocked.

"Seriously," I shot back. "You seem to have a thing for cops lately." Careful to avoid bumping the camera, I leaned in the driver's side door and put his car in neutral. I pushed, hoping that my chosen line of conversation was distracting Kay from seeing what I was doing.

"What's that supposed to mean?" she asked a little too quickly.

The patrol car picked up speed due to its weight and slowly rolled into a tree. It was far enough. "It means what it means. You and Officer Dahl seem to have an unwilling connection."

Even without seeing her face, I could sense the pout I'd find there. "I can't help it if I like looking, but that doesn't mean I'm interested in touching."

"Uh-huh," I teased, simultaneously unraveling some fishing line and cutting it with Bingham's cigarette lighter. That done, I took the protective foil off the next object I had brought: a lovely little pepper bomb.

I knew if given the choice, Kay would have preferred using the pepperball gun on this guy, and I was going to give her something better—even though she would never know about it. By the book, the dart Kay had shot the officer with should take someone out for three to four hours. If that turned out to be the case, we would be well out of his reach. But what if he woke up early?

Either way, that's what this present was for. I tied fishing line to both ends of the pepper bomb and then connected the free ends to the steering wheel and the inside door handle. As soon Officer Bingham woke and opened the door, boom! An obscenely potent pepper spray would fill his car and hopefully distract him from reaching for any communication equipment inside.

Which reminded me . . .

Making sure the trap was set, I returned to Bingham's unconscious form and took the cell phone from his side.

"Wow, I'm a cop shooter," Kay said, still looking at him. "For the rest of my life, if someone asks, I have to say I've shot a cop."

I paused, feeling a moment of regret for letting her take the shooter position. "Are you okay?"

A grin spread across her face. "And when I tell them, no one is going to believe me."

"Oh, I think they're more likely to believe that than your childhood nickname of 'One-Shot Katie,' " I said, heading back to the cruiser and throwing the phone on the passenger seat.

The corners of her nose curled up, as if she had just smelled something bad. "Yeah, let's just keep that little tidbit between us, shall we?" She was taking everything quite well.

"Well, we've lost valuable time. Let's saddle up and get a move on."

"This reminds me of college," Kay mused from out of the

blue, still watching Officer Bingham.

I hesitated in my response, not knowing what memories in particular she was recalling.

She didn't move. "Seriously, we're just going to leave him like this?"

I ventured a smile. "You want to write something on his forehead?"

"Got a marker?"

I did and tossed it to her from the car. "Hurry."

Whatever she wrote, it didn't take her long, and soon we were pulling out of our little nook and on our way back to the freeway. I wanted to leave what we had done behind us, but Kay's smile was so goofy, I had to ask.

"What's got you so happy?"

She looked at me, her smile exuberant. "Call me a dork, but I totally feel like Thelma and Louise right now."

TWENTY-EIGHT

THE CLOCK MOVED closer to noon, and the next hour passed quietly. No more cops and no more tails. It made me nervous.

After we exited I-15, a helicopter appeared once and then again three minutes later. When it passed a third time, I pulled off the freeway onto a dirt road that led to a small patch of trees.

Kay had picked up on it too. "What do you think the helicopter means?"

I reached into one of the packs behind my seat and pulled out a police scanner. "With any luck, this will tell us."

After some trial and error, we found the frequency the Idaho police were using and listened in. It took a bit of creative thought since neither of us knew their codes, but a picture finally came together.

"They're making a barricade," Kay said. "It's just ahead of us, and they're looking for your car. You have Utah plates on here right now?"

"Not for long," I said and got out to head to the trunk. A minute later Kay joined me.

"Oregon?" she asked when she saw the new plates. "Is that going to be enough, Rhea? I mean, think about it. They're not just going to let us by because our plates are different. They know what we look like. Don't you think we need some help?"

The question sounded very leading, so I stopped unscrewing my plates and looked at her. "What are you talking about?"

Her eyes were immediately guilty. "Don't hate me."

"What is it, Kay?"

"You'll thank me later."

I stood. "Out with it!"

She swallowed. "Dahl and Ty are behind us."

"What?" I actually yelled the word

"Like, wa-ay behind us, considering how fast you've been driving. But stopping for that cop helped."

I felt mixed emotions at this news. "How do they know where we are?"

"I've been texting them from the beginning. Once when we got on the freeway, once in the gas station, and again when I went into the woods to shoot that cop. And just now."

"How did it seem like a good idea to involve them, Kay? We left them behind for a reason."

"But Dahl's a cop!" she explained. "Don't you—"

"Being a cop means he has to follow protocol, Kay. He has rules. Technically, I think he may have to arrest me, and you're leading him straight here!"

"He won't arrest you," she snapped. "He's going rogue. You saw his profile. He's former military! He has skills! And I wasn't comfortable leaving Ty at that hotel. After talking to him last night, I knew he was going to do something. Connecting him with Dahl seemed like the right thing to do. They're the ones who decided to follow."

"Of course they did," I grumbled.

"I don't mind the backup, Rhea! It's my life too."

There wasn't time to talk about this. What was done was done, and it was best if all those in harm's way came together.

"Text them and find out where they are. You're right. We can use them to get through the barricade."

I put the Oregon plates back and grabbed another set.

"Montana now?" Kay said while texting.

"They're registered under the name Sam Stone," I explained. "The name isn't gender specific, so it's the best one to use."

"Stone, huh?" she mused. "How many of these extra plates do you have?"

"Only about five or so."

"Well, that's handy," she said and left it at that.

By the time I had the new plates on and was removing the screws to change the VIN, Kay had gotten her response. "They say they're forty minutes behind us."

What were they driving? That was seriously good time on their side. "Good. That will give us some time to redecorate my car." I threw her a can of spray paint.

"We're painting it?" she asked with distaste.

"It's chalk paint. It washes right off, so let's just hope the sky stays as blue as it is right now."

Intrigued, she shook the can and sprayed a line of black on my silver factory job. "Kind of smoky," she noted. "It might just work."

After twenty minutes of painting, Kay's phone beeped with a text. She opened it.

"They think they're close and want to know where we are."

"Tell them to look for a dirt road leading to a pocket of trees on their right. I'll finish up here. You go to the entrance of this little grove and make sure they don't pass us accidentally."

"Sounds good," she agreed and jogged off.

The can in my hand went dry. As I reached for a new can from the trunk, I shook my head, trying to keep my mind from processing too much of the situation. I had to prevent a nervous breakdown at all costs.

Less than a week ago, the biggest things on my mind had been whether or not to train for a triathlon and how to get my boyfriend to take things to the next level. Now I was running from the henchmen of a secret society that didn't like me getting into their business any more than I liked being in it.

What made the situation worse was that I didn't even know if I was making the right move by going up to Wyoming. It was after noon and the clock was ticking, but if everything worked out with Ty and Dahl helping out, it was likely I would get to Donald Smith's house in plenty of time. That much, at least, I could be grateful for.

It was almost over—once we made it through the barricade ahead, anyway. That was all I had to worry about now: the barricade. I couldn't think about the past, my best friend, my boyfriend, or the well-intentioned former missionary who was in protective custody somewhere, rather than professing his undying love to a girl named Marissa Green.

If I thought about anything but the barricade, I might snap.

Hearing the crunch of tires nearby, I stood to greet my friends but they never came into view. After another moment, I realized the sound of tires was moving away from both me and the highway. I felt my stomach go uneasy. What was going on?

Then I heard another set of tires move the same direction, and then another. Three cars. Dahl must have realized he had tails when he stopped to pick up Kay and was leading them away from where I parked.

Good man.

I ran to my car and got my cell phone to call Kay.

"Rhea," she whispered before the phone even finished ringing once. "It's the truck and the Buick. They found Dahl and tailed him here. I don't know how, but they're right behind us."

"It's okay," I whispered back. "Get out of their sight and run my direction. I'll get the guns and meet you halfway, okay? All you have to do is run."

I listened as she relayed my instructions to Dahl. "What kind of guns?" I heard him say, and Kay was smart enough not to answer. "We've just got to get to Rhea, okay?" Kay hissed. "These guys tried to run us' off the road an hour ago. They mean business."

"They what?" Ty jumped in.

I heard another set of tires coming from the freeway. Then another.

"Kay," I interrupted. "Our friends in the Impala and Mazda are here too. Do you understand me? Ditch the car, start running, and don't hang up until we find each other."

"Maybe we should—"

"Run!" I commanded as loudly as I dared, and apparently they all heard me.

I followed my own advice, stopping by the car for my arsenal, and sprinted through the small meadow in an arc-shaped path to where I believed my friends were. Hearing on the phone that they were still in the car was enough to make me want to scream. They were sitting ducks there.

I ran until Dahl's Dodge came into sight and then ducked behind a tree and began unpacking my assortment of weapons. The tranq gun was already loaded with a full clip, minus one. It took two seconds to ready each of my pepper-ball guns and a little longer for the bean bag gun. I eyed the .45. Real guns with real bullets. I didn't know if I could handle knowing that one of them had even been aimed at a person, not to mention fired in that position.

Hearing the approach of rushing footsteps, I peeked around to get a look.

"Rhea! Where are you?" Kay's voice huffed from my phone as I watched her, Ty, and Dahl stay low behind the brush separating them from their four tails.

"A little to your right," I instructed. I looked around for a landmark and didn't find an obvious one. "You're about twenty yards away. I'm behind a tree . . . a little more to the right."

Ty and Dahl were following her lead, but I couldn't see anyone behind them. Where were the men in the other four cars?

"Next tree on your left," I instructed. Two seconds later Kay was panting in front of me and holding her hand out for a gun. I handed her the pepper-ball gun, but she shook her head and pointed to the tranquilizer gun. I didn't argue. I just handed it to her with the extra magazine I had for reloading.

"Where are they?" I asked as Ty and Dahl showed up. Hugs and greetings would have to be saved for later.

Kay indicated Dahl with her thumb. "Dahl made a few funky moves. They're coming, though."

I nodded, handing Ty and Dahl the pepper-ball guns. "We're the distraction and Kay puts them to sleep. Got it?"

Dahl did not like that idea at all. "Is that a tranq gun she's got? No way! I should have that."

"Don't you have a gun?" Kay asked, holding the tranq gun hostage.

"It's in the car," he admitted, which surprised me. He must have seen my expression, because he added defensively. "It digs in when I drive."

"Um, they're coming, guys," Ty warned.

"We're spreading out," I instructed. "How many do you see, Ty?"

"Six, so far."

Six? Where had the extra two come from? "Fine. We're going to run about ten yards together under the cover of the trees we've got, and then we're going to split. Kay, you stay central and out of sight. Ty, you go right, I'm left, and Dahl will go center as well. We want to spread them out and pick them off. Kay, everyone of those guys gets a dart, whether we've hit them or not. Got it?"

She nodded and Dahl predictably objected.

"Shouldn't someone who's trained—"

"Go!" I hissed, and neither Ty nor Kay hesitated, both running straight ahead with me. Dahl was the last one off the line, but was quick to catch up. Not far behind us, voices began calling out, and someone even shot off a round that flew who knew where.

When I called for us to split, everyone went the direction they were told. Alone, I circled back toward the men, praying that Dahl would do what I believed he would do and protect Kay. My second hope was that Ty went far enough to the right that no one would ever find him. Dahl was a cop and former military. I wouldn't feel bad if he came under fire. He had trained for moments like these, whereas Ty was flying blind, sucked into this situation by the mere fact that he had the wrong girlfriend.

I headed back to where I had left my backpack, wishing I had one of the other guns. I had planned on having the tranquilizer, but Kay had thrown me off by asking for it, and before I knew it, I had handed off both of the guns that would have been my second choice. I could only hope that the short-nosed, rifle-shaped beanbag gun was effective on mid-range targets if I was going to take any of these men down.

As expected, the men had found my backpack and two of them were leaning over it. I raised my gun to shoot one of them, when he suddenly crumpled. The man next to him and another one nearby saw this happen and raised their guns to aim off to my left. One guy looked more focused than the other, so I shot him, amazed and pleased when the bag hit him squarely in the face. When I looked back to the other man by my bag, he was already down. A split second later, the bright yellow dart of Kay's tranq gun appeared in the chest of the man I had just downed.

Three down in under a minute. If Kay had been with me, she would have been going off about girl power.

But there were at least three more guys to go.

The sound of gunfire to my left had me sprinting again, and I worried because it was in the vicinity of where Kay must have been. I heard the purr of a pepperball gun, some screams, and then silence.

That's four, I thought, just as I noticed some tracks in the dirt and heard a voice yell, "Dive!"

I did and was pelted by the spraying bark of a tree behind me as it was hit by a bullet. Hearing footsteps draw closer, I rolled into the cover of a bush, aimed through it, and fired twice. One bag hit the guy high in the chest and the other below his belt.

He was hyperventilating every foul word I'd ever heard, and then some, when a dart appeared in his leg from out of nowhere. He settled down quickly after that.

That was five, and number six was probably headed our direction.

Staying low, I moved toward the center without a sound. When I was going through my outdoor photography phase, Kay always teased me that learning how to stalk animals for pictures was a useless skill, but it was coming in handy now. Months of tedious practice rendered my footfalls silent as I closed in on Kay and Dahl's turf. Then I heard the sound I dreaded the most: gunfire coming from Ty's direction.

Far less cautious now, I flew toward the right and was joined by Kay after about fifty yards. We didn't speak, and I didn't even think to ask about Dahl as shots continued to fire. A long, loud scream was enough to propel me ahead of Kay and recklessly into the trees.

When my head came over a slight rise, the only thing I registered was that I did not know the man I was looking at before shooting him squarely in the back. He fell forward, turning and trying to empty his gun on me on his way down. That's when I noticed his eyes were sealed shut from a pepperball. With him safely writhing on the ground, I moved forward and kicked his gun away from him.

That was six.

"Ty!" I called out. "Ty, are you okay?"

"Okay," he shouted back, out of sight and from a decent distance. Thank heaven!

Kay appeared over the ridge and approached the man without hesitation. "It's sleepy time," she cooed, and fired. "That's six," she said, her mind the same place mine was. "Are we sure that's it? Maybe one or two stayed behind to be back up."

"Maybe," I agreed. "We'll have to be careful."

"Okay, you two!" Dahl boomed in his most intimidating voice as he came over the same ridge Kay and I had. "What in the world just happened?" His next move was to hit the ground, however, as Kay and I both took aim behind him.

The man behind Dahl was the man I remembered from the truck. He had been smart, stalking us until we reformed into a pod so he could shoot us all at once, but even though his gun was aimed at Kay, ready to fire, he had hesitated when he found only three of us.

Without a word or cue from anyone we found ourselves in an interesting deadlock: Kay and I standing and aiming at F150 Man, Dahl on the ground doing the same, and F150 Man choosing Kay as his target.

"Put your weapon down!" Dahl called out, sounding like the cop that he was. His order was ignored.

"Where's the other guy?" the man asked me with complete calm. And why shouldn't he be calm? He had the only lethal weapon in the circle. I might as well have armed my friends with squirt guns.

I didn't blink. "What other guy?"

"There were four of you. Where's your boyfriend?"

I glanced at Kay, who was smirking as she held her gun steady.

"I hope he's not feeling like a hero," he called out into the trees. "Because I don't think your friend here is ready to die. One move and I shoot, so why don't you all put your weapons down."

We may have only been armed with powerful toys, but none of us moved.

"You think I'm kid—"

He was interrupted mid-sentence by the ring of a pepper-ball gun to his right, and his arm flinched to aim at the sound in reflex. Kay and I fired simultaneously, and while I'm sure Dahl did the same, his hopper had come loose when he hit the ground. F150 Man fired in reflex when my bag hit him in the forehead, but the shot went high and wide as his body fell back with a yellow dart in the neck.

"Way to get down," Kay said, stepping forward and offering Dahl a hand up. He ignored her hand and got up fuming.

"Who in the world is after you, Ms. Jensen?"

"You're really asking her that after what happened yesterday?" Kay said lazily, checking her magazine.

"I was just involved in a shoot-out!" he snapped. "Are—"

"That's not entirely accurate," Kay interrupted sweetly. "It's not like you actually fired your gun."

She was gloating, plain and simple, and loving every moment of it. Dahl clearly wasn't. I jumped in before he could say anything else.

"Which reminds me, thank you to whoever told me to dive back there."

Kay lost all interest in Dahl. "You mean from that shot that nearly took your head off?"

I nodded. "That would be the one."

Her face became uncharacteristically gaunt. "I thought you were hit when you went down, and I'm sure that guy did too. He was perched up in a pine tree just waiting for you. I didn't see him till he popped out after you went down."

"Me neither," Dahl added.

I was confused. "Then how did you know to tell me to dive?"

Kay shrugged. "I wish I could take the credit for that one, but I can't."

Dahl looked equally baffled. "I didn't say anything either, Rhea."

I felt a shiver go through me.

"But let's get back on topic here," Dahl said, stabbing his finger at Kay. "Where did you learn to shoot like that?"

Oh, Ken Dahl. Apparently he had a bit of chauvinism mired into him. Wouldn't Kay have fun with that.

"Who do you think taught me to shoot?" I asked, saving her from having to answer.

"Wha—" he looked between us in disbelief, his eyes finally settling on Kay as if Reporter Barbie came with horns and a tail. "You taught Rhea to shoot?"

"Freshman year at UCLA," Kay replied with a hint of a drawl. I smiled at her, checking out my arm when Ty appeared from out of nowhere.

"You're hurt," were his first words as he rushed to help me inspect my right arm.

"Just scratches," I said, afraid to let him too near me. It was time to move, and if I let him attend to me I might just indulge in a little dawdling. Just like tears, boyfriends were for after you made it through the fire, not for hugging while you were still in it.

"Nice distraction fire. Glad you're safe," I said, hating that I sounded completely relieved.

"I was circling to make sure no one else was sneaking up on us." His eyes fell on where chips of bark still stuck out of my arm from my near miss. "Here, let me make a bandage for this."

I stepped away, already feeling volunteer tears lining up for the exit. "I've got it covered. We've got to keep moving. We've got a barricade ahead and four hours to make an appointment."

"But, Rhea," Dahl said, stepping forward. "In a few hours, these guys are going to wake up, and they're still going to want to kill you. Leaving them here unconscious accomplishes nothing."

"You want to call it in?" I asked. "These guys are connected, Ken. More connected than you can probably imagine. We hand them over, and they'll be woken up even quicker so they can share what they know."

He eyed the man who'd nearly shot Kay, clearly debating.

"All I care about is getting to Teton Village before seven. As long as you don't get in the way of that, do whatever you want and take Ty with you."

Dahl moved in, pressuring me. "And what's in Teton Village?"

I stood my ground. "That's none of your business, but if you'd like to help me get there, I'd be grateful."

The mental struggle he was going through as we faced off was fierce, but when it was over, he said the words I wanted to hear. Or at least a version of them.

"I should drive your car. I'm a cop and have more of a chance getting through a barricade. We'll put all your stuff in my Dodge, and Ty'll drive that."

I turned to Ty. "You up for that?"

He nodded, trying not to look as hurt and confused as he felt. I was all business and willing to leave him after his effort to join me. There wasn't another guy on the planet who could roll with my punches like Ty could.

"That takes care of the cars, but where do we go?" Kay asked. "It's us they're looking for."

"The trunk," Dahl said.

"What? With all of Rhea's luggage?"

Dahl stepped forward and touched her arm. "Kay, it's the—"

"Kathryn!" Kay snapped, her eyes dangerous. "My name is *Kathryn.*"

"I'm sorry, it just seems natural—"

"Everyone else in the world calls me Kathryn, and you will too."

Dahl looked stunned by the rebuke, but Kay was not about to apologize as she stalked away. For whatever reason, Dahl chose not to take a hint. "What does someone have to do in order to be special enough to call you Kay?"

There were only a handful of people in the world who knew that was probably the most terribly worded question someone could ask her, and I knew it was time to step in. I ran forward, stopping Dahl from pursuing Kay.

"Get my bag, will you? Take Ty with you, and I'll go with Kay and make sure there's no one left to shoot us."

Without waiting for a response, I ran to catch up with Kay.

"Slow down," I soothed. "We still may not be the only ones here."

She stopped and leaned against a tree. "You'd think I'd be over it."

I let out a slow breath and looked back to make sure Ty and Dahl couldn't see us. "I know, Kay, but he doesn't. How could he?"

She gave a sniffle, although her eyes betrayed nothing. "You didn't tell Ty, did you? I can tell because he looked as confused as Ken."

I flashed an apologetic smile as I reached out to rub her arm. "It's not my story to tell."

"Yeah. Of course," Kay said. She hugged me and changed the subject. "How come you almost die so much?"

Needless to say, that, of all possible questions, was not the one I was expecting. I had no response for it.

"Remember in L.A. last April when you were in that trunk and those guys tried to blow your head off?"

Giving her no points for delicacy, I nodded. She pulled away and looked at me.

"Well, if you can get in a trunk after all that, then I guess I can too. Let's go."

My mind was still recalling the sensation of a gun barrel being pressed against my head when I realized Kay was marching back to the car. I followed behind her, gun raised just in case, with Ty and Dahl less than a minute behind us. I made quick work of collecting the guns, after which we all piled into Dahl's Dodge, accompanied by an ominous silence.

"Hey, Ken, do you think any of those men saw my car when you pulled up?" I asked.

"No way," he replied. "I was looking for it and I didn't see it."

"Good, because we've changed the look a little bit, and with any luck that will help you out."

"What did you change?" he asked.

"New color, new . . . plates."

"What? I'll be driving under phony plates?"

"Calm down," I said. "They're registered under the name Sam Stone for a Audi in Montana. It will all check out if they run them."

"That's illegal, Rhea," he growled.

"Yes, I'm aware of that. Thanks."

He turned to look at me, clearly uneasy. "Besides, they can still identify your car by the VIN."

I fought the urge to clear my throat and kept my face expressionless. "That won't be an issue."

Dahl was about to let me know how little he liked that answer when Kay burst in.

"Sorry about yelling at you back there," she said to Dahl. "That was rude and I'm sorry."

He still looked uncomfortable, but in a different way. "Me too. For whatever I said back there. I'm still not sure."

I led the group back to my car. Even I was impressed when I saw the effect of the changes I had made to the car.

"It doesn't even look like yours anymore," Ty praised.

"Let's hope not. Now, I think Dahl should go ahead and put some distance between us. Hopefully after talking to him, they'll think they spotted the wrong R8 and take down the barricade. We'll wait here a full ten minutes before following. Dahl, if something goes wrong, text us any kind of message at all. Sound good?"

"Got it," he said, snatching my keys. "Now let's get your stuff out of here and into my trunk."

We made quick work and then Dahl was gone. My heart actually hurt watching him pull away with my baby. After today, I was pretty sure I would never be able to bring myself to sell the thing.

"I don't like the idea of you two in the trunk," Ty said as soon as Dahl was gone.

"Me neither," I agreed. Kay looked surprised. "We're not going with you, Ty, but I didn't trust Dahl to know that in case he calls all this in."

Both Ty and Kay looked uneasy, but it was Ty who spoke. "So what do we do?"

I looked to Kay. "You up for a jog?"

She nodded.

"Okay, then this is what we're going to do . . . "

TWENTY-NINE

"I **WISH TY HAD** a tall brother," Kay heaved, running along side me. "But in the off-chance we actually survive the rest of this day, I give my consent for you to marry this one."

I leapt over a small shrub that was in our way. "Glad to have your approval."

She kept going. "He totally read your mind about the trunk situation too. I watched him do it. And the way he didn't get all macho when you asked him to leave your arm alone? Man, why can't I find a man like that?"

"Because you like men who pamper you."

Since it was just the two of us, she didn't argue. "Maybe I do, but don't go spreading that around."

We'd run about a mile alongside the highway. It was 2:15, and I was trying not to freak out about how time seemed to be disappearing. Kay and I still had four miles ahead of us, and the clock was ticking. Still, stressing Kay out by yelling at her to go faster was not going to help, so I tried to do things that would—like keeping her mind occupied as I pressed her pace. After all, she didn't train for moments like these. I did.

"How much farther?" she puffed.

I looked at the screen of my GPS. "Don't know yet," I lied. "Ty still seems to be at the road block."

"It's been like ten minutes now. What if he doesn't get through?"

I sped up a little. "Then things are gonna get harder."

She swore and sped up with me.

Five minutes later, Ty's car was moving again, and two minutes after that, the little dot on my screen stopped a half a mile short of where I had expected it to.

"Don't move!" I told the dot, and Kay drifted closer.

"Where is he?"

I showed her. "If he stays where he is then we only have two and a half more miles."

"Don't move!" Kay repeated, stabbing her finger at the blinking dot on my handheld.

We trucked on, our mantra ironically being "Don't move!" as we narrowed the distance between us and the car. The dot obeyed and didn't move.

When we were about half a mile away, the trees thickened, giving us cover as we ran back in the direction of the highway. Ty had parked the vehicle on our side of the street, on a small dirt path that didn't look too popular.

"He stashed the car out of sight and got Dahl to leave without us?" Kay marveled.

"He's *my* boyfriend," I reminded her, picking the keys up from under the tire and unlocking the car.

"Oh, yeah, he's tailor-made for you, Rhea. I wouldn't dream of having a guy like that. Besides, it was kind of hot to have Dahl all pissed off that he couldn't shoot the bad guys for me."

After a little bit of digging in the car, I found a half-empty bottle of water. Taking off my shirt, I poured some of it on my bloody arm and tried to clean it with the fabric. Kay kept talking.

"Did you notice? He was all . . . protective of me. And he moves so well in those cowboy boots. Not like a city guy but like someone who was raised in them."

My lips formed a sneaky curve. "Are you admitting you like him now?"

"I like having him around when I'm in trouble," she clarified. "Once we get back to Salt Lake, I know he'll just be another anal retentive Mormon cop."

"Such a shame," I mourned, showing her my arm. "Does it look clean?"

"Yeah, but I hope you brought something with long sleeves. It looks nasty. And it's not fair that you have a six-pack just standing there. I can't get one no matter how hard I try."

"Guys don't like six-packs on girls," I said, popping the trunk.

"Even Ty?" she teased.

"Even Ty," I agreed. "He's obsessed with feeding me."

"Good! Someone should be. Just another reason why he's perfect for you."

"Yeah," I said, but was starting to wonder if a woman who led him on crazy adventures like this was perfect for him.

She dabbed and powdered her face as she waited for me as I used the I Can't . . . I'm Mormon shirt as a rag to clean my wounds.

"If I'd have known I would be running a 10K, I would have brought a change of clothes," she grumbled.

"Sorry," I said, lamenting putting my own sweaty shirt back on. "Maybe we can buy something when we get there."

"Oh, I bet there's great shopping in Jackson Hole!"

Leave it to Kay to find a silver lining.

"You ready?" I asked. "We're about to find out if all this was worth it."

"We've made it this far," Kay said, giving my injured arm a squeeze. I didn't have the heart to tell her that it hurt. "Lead the way!"

THIRTY

IT TURNED OUT that even after all we'd been through, we still had time to go shopping. Dressed in new threads, we pulled up to the Smith Ranch at five on the nose. All nine-point-four breathtaking acres of the property were framed majestically against the backdrop of jagged peaks. The cloud-covered sky glowed a pale gray that somehow rendered the surrounding grasses even greener. It was gorgeous—almost enough to make me forget what lay behind the door of the equally magnificent ranch home.

As usual, I didn't let my imagination run away with me. It was best to deal with things as they came.

A maid answered Mr. Smith's door and showed us into a rustic sitting room. The stone floor was covered in handmade rugs and animal furs, while heads of indigenous and foreign wildlife graced the log cabin walls, which stretched upward at least two stories. A fire glowed in the fireplace; two reading chairs and a lamp were arranged in front of it. Across the room was a Fazioli piano, while the near side of the room was home to a very nice bar. Off to our left, a spiraling staircase led to a catwalk full of bookshelves and an alcove.

"It smells like leather in here," Kay said, breathing deeply.

I pointed to the heads on the wall.

Her nose crinkled. "Oh. And look at that fireplace. That must be six feet tall! It's gorgeous."

I nodded and kept looking around, my eyes repeatedly being drawn to the catwalk because I knew my sense of self-preservation would want me to look up there later. I couldn't, though. No matter how badly I wanted to, I shouldn't look.

Behind us, the man I recognized from computer images to be Donald Smith walked in clapping in a way both patronizing and sincere.

"Applaudable work, Ms. Jensen," he said, looking exactly how you might imagine a sixty-one year old billionaire would look on a quiet evening. He was taller than I thought he'd be, standing a few inches above Kay. His full head of silver hair, porcelain veneers, and trim body could have belonged to a man twenty years younger. "Honing in on my passion for property as your 'in,' Ms. Jensen? Genius." He noted us both standing and staring at him in shock and took it in stride. "Oh, did Liesel not ask you to take a seat? I never imagined you would make it this far, but you much be exhausted." He motioned to two overstuffed chairs before lowering into one himself. "Please. Let's talk."

He knew who I was. He knew who Kay was, and he knew that neither of us were real estate agents. Not good.

"May I offer you ladies something to drink?"

To refuse would be a show of distrust.

"A water would be great," I replied, and he looked to Kay.

"You look like you could use some wine," he commented.

"I'll take water for the moment as well," she said.

He walked to nearby bar and served us himself, pouring a double scotch out of a very old, very expensive-looking bottle before rejoining us in the sitting area and handing us each a glass of water. Then he sat and gave the scotch a small sip.

"It's fitting that you're both here," he decided. "You seem to work well as team."

Kay and I shared a look, and I could see the temper flaring in her eyes. I shook my head.

"You know we're not here about the property," I said, looking at him. "Do you know what brought us here?"

"Skill and ingenuity?" he ventured.

Well, maybe a little bit of that. "Oliver Westman."

"Ah, yes," Donald said, setting his scotch aside. "The man who would have your job." The comment was a total curve ball.

"Job?" the word came from Kay's mouth, not mine.

"Yes," he said, motioning to the room in general. "Welcome to your job interview, Ms. Jensen. Here's a hint: you're hired."

I shook my head. "I don't want it."

Donald gave me another one of his patronizing looks. "You don't even know what the job is."

I kept my expression flat. "Considering the interview, I don't care what it is. I'm not interested."

Donald, of course, did not listen to me. The word "no" did not exist in his world. "I need someone over Intermountain West. You were with Elliott in L.A., so you weren't a candidate before, but you'd be perfect in Salt Lake City. Oliver wanted the job too, so I told him to prove to me that he was better than you." His lips turned up in a conniving smile. "He didn't. Not by a long shot."

Strangely enough, that actually cleared up a few things.

"Be that as it may," I replied. "I'm not your girl."

His eyebrows shot up. "So you want Oliver to be over Utah?"

Trick question. "The man is an idiot."

"Well, you've definitely painted him to be one. But can I ask why you didn't just take him out? He tried to kill you. Several times."

My jaw clenched at the memory. "I avoid hurting people if I can. No matter who they are."

He motioned to Kay. "That's where she comes in handy, right?" He sent her knowing smile. "Isn't that right, Ms. Griswold? You're not as shy as your friend when it comes to things like that, are you." It wasn't a question.

Kay flinched, but the fact that he knew her real last name shouldn't have been a shock to her. She'd only changed it six years before and it was public record.

"I'm not an Elliott or an Oliver," I replied. "Neither is Kathryn."

"No, you are uniquely you, Ms. Jensen, which is why I must have you on my team."

Kay tensed and looked at me while I shook my head again. "I won't do it."

He *tsked* me like a child. "Oh, but you just proved that you would, Ms. Jensen. If properly motivated, you'll do anything I ask."

I grew still and our eyes met—him, the smug predator and me, the cornered prey.

"Maybe you won't pull a trigger for me. I can live with that," he mused. "I have no shortage of those who are willing, but you bring a whole different skill set to the table. You're like a ballerina who dances through a gauntlet, leaving the warriors around you broken and bruised. That kind of finesse is rare."

Next to me, I sensed Kay understood the gravity of the situation and could almost hear the wheels in her head spinning, trying to find an escape. Well, mine were too.

Donald kept talking, which was good for me. Everything he told me leveled our playing field a bit. He knew that, and still he talked. I dare say that meant he liked me.

"Once you went off grid, Ms. Jensen, we didn't find you until you came back out, and that is a big deal. I even knew you would go to Dingo for help. We were ready to trace that link, but he caught it too fast." His eyes narrowed on me with meaning. "When I could not find you, you found me, Ms. Jensen.

Tell me what that means."

It means I'm screwed. Absolutely and totally screwed.

"I've retired," I said, clinging to my last straw.

"At twenty-five?" he laughed. "My dear, you've only just begun. And as an added bonus, you've just made me an equal opportunity employer. I've never hired a woman before."

It was wrong that I felt a little proud of that.

"What's the job description?" Kay chimed in, and I reached out too late to hush her. No questions. It sent mixed messages. The answer to his offer had to be a hard no with no curiosity attached. But Donald sensed the shift, and his smile turned downright evil.

"The job is simple: Protect the interests of people I'm invested in, and take down those who work against me. Nothing Rhea here hasn't done for years."

I felt sick. Physically ill. In all those years with Elliott, I'd known the caliber of our client list hadn't been a happy accident, but I never would have guessed I was part of something this sinister.

"Your record is impeccable. Not one failure, even against a peer who fought to oust you."

Suddenly I did have a question. "Why did you allow Oliver to go after the Epsons if this was all a test for me?"

Donald raised an eyebrow. "You made it this far without figuring that out?"

"I get how Kay and I fit in," I said. "But did Mark steal a pledge? The whole suicide thing was totally bizarre."

Donald reached for his scotch again. "I'm afraid that's what happens when you mix your business life with your personal." He took a sip. "Oliver's youngest brother pledged with Epson's society rather than ours. All these years, Oliver had planned on his brother being his apprentice, and then the kid disqualifies himself. When I asked Oliver what task he would accomplish under your nose while you watched on in baffled horror, he said he would expose and take down this fraternity through you two, and get his brother back on track for recruitment. The idea was an interesting one, so why not let him try?"

At last, I had the piece I'd been missing, but Oliver had still made several tactical errors if that had been his main goal.

"Then why buy me off the case?" I was asking too many questions and investing myself in the conversation. Doing so gave Donald power, but I had to know. "That was a huge error."

"Yes and no," Donald replied. "The purpose was to let you start down the road of the investigation and then use the bribe to increase your interest even more. He counted on you feeding the story to Kathryn, thus making you both witless pawns and Oliver a mastermind."

I was even more stunned. "He was basing his success on the lure of reverse psychology?" What an idiot!

Kay was the one sending warning looks now, and I realized she was right. I was making myself look better and better in Donald's eyes with my comments. It was time to shut up.

"All this does not change my answer, Mr. Smith. With respect, I decline your offer. I've found religion since working with Elliott, as you may have heard through the rumor mill."

"I work with Mormons," he said without hesitation, and I knew it was true.

"Mr. Smith, you're not hearing me—"

"No, you're not hearing me, Ms. Jensen. You've already proven you will work for me. Oliver did me the favor of show-ing me what buttons set you into motion. I can blow up houses too, Rhea. I can cause accidents, bankrupt families, or do any-thing that will get you dancing through the next gauntlet. And if you ever turn on me, Rhea?" He reached for his glass with a lazy confidence. "If you ever disappear and start working against me? I won't kill you first. I'll kill your niece, your dad, your family, your boyfriend and his family. Maybe even your missionary houseguest from this week and his new lady friend. I could arrange a car accident. And after they've gone, I'd come get you." He swirled the scotch in his glass, watching me. "You make a single move against me, Ms. Jensen, and I'll do all that without blinking. Or you could just take the job."

I could feel Kay looking at me and wished she wouldn't. We had more power if the two of us stared Donald down unfazed.

"Or you could just keep The Fours a men-only fraternity and let me walk."

With the utterance of these two magic words—their own insider term that I would never have known if it wasn't for Dingo—I could have sworn the temperature in the room dropped a full twenty degrees.

"It alarms me that after all this, I've still failed to give you enough credit, Ms. Jensen," he said softly. "Where did you learn that name?"

"Does it matter?"

"Yes," he breathed. "Very much."

"Let me refuse the job and I'll tell you," I offered.

The way his eyes fastened on me, I knew he was considering pulling the trigger on me and Kay right then. And when a predator stares you in the eye, there's only one thing to do: stare right back. The moment your eyes retreat, they attack.

His eyes held mine for a solid ten seconds.

"A person like you can be hard to deal with, Ms. Jensen," he mused. "Normal rules don't fit you well. In a way, it's a rare treat."

I could roll with that.

His eyes continued to analyze me before crinkling in amusement. "Okay, let's say I bite. Name one reason for me to change my mind, Ms. Jensen."

As long as he kept calling me Ms. Jensen, he was considering shooting me. That was my gut assessment, at least. And his question had no good intentions behind it. He was handing me a rope to hang myself with. Whatever I said, he was going to turn it against me. Yet knowing that, I had to answer. And the answer had to be good, preferably playing into any prejudices Donald Smith might have about me—or women in general. It had to be something that weakened me in his estimation.

"I want to get married," I blurted before the words even registered in my mind. It was as if someone had said them for me. "I want to have babies."

To Kay's credit, she stopped her jaw before it dropped, but I'm sure Donald sensed her shock, which of course, undermined me.

The man threw his head back and laughed, but I pushed on anyway, trying to fuel whatever spark of doubt I may have lit in his mind.

"Do you really want a housewife as one of your right-hand people, Mr. Smith? Or worse yet, a pregnant mother? Who would take me seriously?"

Donald's laugh simmered so he could take a drink. Not the reaction I was looking for. "Nice try, Ms. Jensen, but Elliott profiled you before we accepted you for training. You are a confirmed loner with advanced thanatophobia and paralyzing fear of commitment. The likelihood of you choosing to commit to a marriage and bring children to it is virtually nonexistent."

At the time those findings had been absolutely true. They still pretty much were, but I needed him to doubt his on findings.

"I was practically a teenager when you trained me," I argued.

"And we've retested you every year since."

What? How? I struggled to find how they'd slipped into my mind. For the moment, it didn't matter. "Have you tested me since I got baptized?"

We both knew the answer to that. Nope, they sure hadn't.

"People change when they find God," I said, and again, the words found me. "My priorities are different now. I want different things." Which was true, if you counted not knowing what I wanted at all. But more important than whether or not I was telling the truth or not was the fact that Donald's eyes showed a small crack of reconsideration. I had to plow on.

"I pray now, Mr. Smith. I read the scriptures and tie quilts at the local hospital." What else did Mormons do? I thought back on my dates with my ex-boyfriend, Chad. "I volunteer at food banks and homeless shelters and have only taken one case since I became a Mormon to help a woman who was being terrorized. This is who I am now, no matter what your outdated test results tell you, Mr. Smith. As unique as my skill set is, why would you want someone like me working for you?"

I waited for his response to gauge how effective this argument was on him. Not very, based on the amused expression in his eyes. "You want me to believe all this? That you would throw your career away and live happily as a homemaker?"

My stomach clenched at the thought, but my mouth ignored it. "It's who I am now, Mr. Smith."

He remained amused. "So you much imagine that your current boyfriend, Ty Kimball, is the prince charming that will make all these dreams come true."

I swallowed, not liking that Donald knew Ty's name. "A girl can hope."

"Miss Griswold," he said, looking to Kay again. "What do you think of Rhea's current boyfriend?"

She hesitated, looking between us, but I gave her no cue. "I think he's fantastic," she confessed.

"In your estimation, could your friend do any better?"

Kay swallowed nervously, but I knew her answer. "Not a chance. He's the only guy she would marry."

"Then I should kill him," he said simply. "Problem solved."

Panic gripped me in a choke hold as Kay sent me a look of terror.

"But now I'm intrigued," he continued. "I have millions of dollars invested in research that I place a lot of stock in. That same research tells me that Rhea here would rather be set on fire or thrown off a cliff than be confined to a domestic existence and live out her life like her mother."

The words hit me like the unapologetic slap that they were. He narrowed his eyes on me. "You know it, Rhea. You'll leave anyone you marry, whether you want to or not. You'll abandon any child you have, and you won't be able to help it."

An invisible band wrapped itself around my chest and squeezed in at his words.

"Isn't that right?" he pressed.

I couldn't deny it. I was pretty sure I couldn't speak at all, so I focused on maintaining eye contact. Next to me, Kay stayed silent.

"I see that I am right, but in the name of fair play, we shall do this, Ms. Jensen." His eyes crinkled, enjoying the idea forming in his mind. "You have six months to marry Ty Kimball. If you're not married by this day next March, we will meet again and you will accept my offer. If you refuse again, I'll kill Ty Kimball. I don't care if you break up with him the moment you walk out my front door tonight. If you're unmarried in six months and refuse to join me, he dies."

Next to me, Kay's stalwartness melted. I looked at her briefly and noticed her eyes had filled with tears.

"But if you truly defy the profiling I so frequently rely on to make my most important decisions and find the nerve to get married, we shall meet again in six months to re-profile you. Then we'll see what is to be done for you to repay me for your current wealth based on my investment in you." He picked up his scotch and swirled it. "And I assure you, it will be creative."

Kay had stopped breathing. Her hands gripped the arms of her chair so hard that her veins stuck out.

"This is my only offer, Ms. Jensen. You proved Oliver to be incompetent. Will you prove my research to be flawed as well?"

It was the only choice, wasn't it? I had to take the six months to regroup. What else could I do? Join him right then and be bound to the darkest of businesses for the rest of my life?

Taking six months to regroup was my only option.

The whole thing about killing Ty freaked me out, but I wouldn't let that happen. I would make sure he never got hurt, romantically linked or not.

"You are offering me a chance at normal life. Is that correct, Mr. Smith?" I clarified.

"Yes. To prove to us both that you will not take it. To prove to you that no matter how much you think you love this man, it is not enough to overcome the fears that brought you to me in the first place."

Nothing more needed to be said. Even Kay understood why he was so confident as she turned to me with eyes of pity.

"So go. Run back to your men," Donald said, standing and addressing both of us now. "And try to feel half as alive in their arms as you did on the road here today." He motioned the direction of the door. "I'll walk you out."

None of us spoke. There was nothing more to say as Liesel rushed to the door and opened it for us.

"I'll see you in six months, Ms. Jensen," he said at the door.

"And until then, your men leave me alone? Even Oliver?"

He nodded. "You have my word."

"Then see I'll you in six months," I agreed and led Kay out.

"Ms. Jensen?" he called after me. Hatred boiled in me so deep that it took all my self-control to turn and face him.

"Yes?"

"If by some miracle you actually follow through with your claim, have sons," he said, smiling broadly. "Lots of sons. Drive safely!" The door shut.

THIRTY-ONE

IT WAS A miracle, but I made it all the way to Dahl's car before throwing up in the grass. Kay came to my side, giddy to have survived at all.

"I can't believe we're alive!" she rambled. "The second we walked in and he knew who we were, I thought we were goners. Once we got past Oliver's men, he let us walk right in. He thought he had you, but you got him to doubt! I can't believe you did that! And marriage? Holy crap! Where did that come from?"

Hands on my knees, eyes trained on the ground, I didn't answer. Donald Smith probably had cameras trained on me, documenting my reaction and mocking me. I chose not to care.

"You can never do a story on a secret society ever again," I warned her. Donald hadn't said as much, but she knew way too much to walk away unscathed if she even touched the subject in the media.

She shrugged. "Don't you get it, Rhea? We're alive! You did the absolute gutsiest thing in the world and got away with it! I had so much adrenaline shooting through my system back there that my teeth started chattering. We were one word away from dead. Did you feel it?"

Yes. I did.

"You've always had a way with powerful men . . . or men in general. You get them and they get you, but I nearly died when you brought up marriage! How are you going to tell Ty?"

"I'm not," I said quickly.

She grew still. "Rhea, you have to."

"Only if he proposes," I said. "Otherwise what happened in there has nothing to do with him."

"But he—"

"He should not be manipulated into marrying me just so I don't have to deal with Donald Smith!" I snapped, and we stared each other down. "He can't sign his life over to me to try and save me, Kay. He has to make that choice on his own."

"In six months? Without knowing a clock is ticking?" she objected. "That's not fair!"

"Neither is life, but that's how it's going to play out so promise me you won't interfere. Promise me!"

She faltered, clearly disagreeing with me. "Fine," she agreed at last, moving to the passenger side. "It's your stupid life."

"Thank you," I said, straightening myself. My stomach still felt uneasy, but there was nothing left in it. When I got in the car, Kay dug through the glove compartment, where Dahl's gun sat unused, and found a pack of gum.

"You need this," she said, pulling out a piece. "I can't share a car with vomit breath."

I took it and chewed it thankfully as we drove down the massive driveway and the automated gate opened to let us out.

* * *

"I have to confess something," Kay said when we hit the road.

"What's that?"

She sent me a cautious look. "If I didn't know you, I'm

pretty sure I would have talked myself out of believing in God by now. But I don't think I'll ever be able to do that as long as you're around, since your butt is always being saved in miraculous ways. I haven't met a person in my life that is half as charmed as you—and don't pretend you haven't noticed that everything miraculously works out in your favor, no matter what situation you get yourself into!"

There was no denying the entire day had been a miracle, so I let Kay give credit where credit was due as we drove the short distance over to Jackson Hole, where Ty and Ken were waiting.

"I need a man," Kay muttered in abrupt change of subject. She was processing. "It's not fair that you have a boyfriend."

Beneath her gripe I heard what she really meant. She'd wanted to kiss Officer Dahl from the first moment she laid eyes on him, and after looking Death in the face, she was going to do whatever she pleased. Unless he ducked and ran for cover, Ken Dahl would find himself going to lip to lip with Reporter Barbie in about three minutes.

But neither of us said that out loud.

"There they are!" she cried in obvious relief. "Under the, uh, antler thing. That's disgusting!" And it pretty much was. A massive arch sculpted entirely of antlers marked the entrance to some sort of park. But underneath it stood two perfectly huggable hunks of men. "Pull over! Pull over!"

I slowed to a stop and Kay was out of the car before the ground had stopped moving under her feet. To my surprise, and probably everyone else's, she flew to Ty first.

"It's so good to see you again," she cried, forcing him to catch her mid-air.

I stepped out of the car and watched as she whispered something into Ty's ear. It was a move she obviously didn't want me to see, but there was only one thing I cared about her telling him. As long as it wasn't that, I'd let anything slide.

When Ty set her down, she turned to Dahl and approached.

"Don't take this personally," she warned. "You just happen to be the only unattached man in the vicinity, and deep down I know you want it." Then, in a move far bolder than any I had made that day, she pulled him into a kiss that would win her an MTV Movie Award.

At first, Dahl appeared stunned, but he didn't pull away. In fact, his actions were quite to the contrary.

Ty moved to me, so that only my door stood as a barrier between us.

"Maybe now he'll finally shut up," he said through a cautious smile.

"Was he worried?" I asked, using the question as an excuse not to look at Ty.

"That's an understatement, but that's over now. How are you?"

Why did you have to ask? I wanted to scream as razor-sharp tears fought their way from my eyes. *You promised*, they seemed to say. *You promised that when this was all over you'd let us out!* I tried telling them to wait five more minutes when Ty saw the struggle and quickly skirted the door between us and wrapped his arms around me.

"Let it out," he whispered. "It's my turn to be strong now, okay?"

He had no idea. Here he was, being all perfect when he had no idea that we were doomed from the start. But still, I couldn't help holding on to his neck for all I was worth and sobbing.

The last time my mortality was called into question, all I could think of after were the regrets I would have had if I had died that night. This time, I regretted what my future would be because I had cheated death. I regretted what it had cost me, because I couldn't ask for a better man than Ty, but I had no right to ask him to deal with what I'd walked into.

But that talk could come later. For now, I could hold on tight. Both of us needed that, and I was done being stoic for that day.

By the time Kay started feigning disinterest in Dahl, I couldn't have cared less about the words coming out of their mouths. I was kissing my boyfriend, thank you very much, and considering I might be doing so for the last time, I wasn't pulling any punches.

THIRTY-TWO

TY RODE WITH me until we got into Idaho, where we stopped to eat. When we were loading back up, I convinced him I needed some alone time and that he needed to go with Dahl and Kay. Despite his extreme reluctance, I got in my car alone.

Instead of stopping in Salt Lake City, I kept going south on I-15. It was three in the morning when I passed through Vegas, and had I been in a healthy frame of mind, I would have gotten a hotel. But I wasn't, so I didn't. I kept on driving to the only place I knew I could go when I felt empty.

The morning sun was gaining heat as I pulled into my father's driveway and, knowing he would be at work, I dragged myself up the stairs, flopped on my bed, and passed out.

A soft knock came on my door at 6:37.

"Rhea?" It was my father's voice, and I forced my eyes open, too tired to realize that we hadn't spoken since I arrived. Being home just felt natural.

"Hmm," I grumbled.

"Sorry to wake you," he said, venturing in. "But I thought I should make sure you were alive."

"Sorry. I didn't mean to sleep this long."

He laughed his agreement. "I was going to wake you last night, but I wasn't—"

My eyes flew open. "Last night?"

He nodded. "You were here when I got home from work last night, and I thought we could go out to dinner, but I wasn't sure when you had pulled in, so I left you alone. You've been asleep for at least twelve hours now, so I figured it was safe to wake you."

I was completely disoriented. "It's 6:37 in the morning?" That meant I had slept through Sunday entirely and missed church. Somehow that seemed appropriate. Part of me felt relief at the knowledge that I still had six more days to digest what had happened before trying to see if church, religion, or faith still applied to people like me.

He smiled. "Yes, it's Monday morning. When did you get in yesterday?"

I leaned back and draped my arm over my eyes. "I plead the Fifth."

He laughed, a full rich sound that made me feel at home. "How about dinner tonight, then? Fancy. It's been a while since I showed my daughter off."

"It's a date, but could we go low key? I don't have a dress."

"Buy one then," he said, crossing the room and kissing the back of my hand. "Be ready by seven sharp, and I'll make sure tonight is memorable."

Properly motivated and knowing that I had plenty of sleep under my belt, I got up and showered. By the time businesses opened, I was on the phone making appointments. I scheduled a massage, facial, and mani-pedi at the spa, and an old friend was able to create some space for a hair appointment at four. My dad asked for fancy, and he was going to get it.

I tried to ignore the fact that I was doomed to remain a spinster who made deals with the devil. Ty had made it clear that he wanted to wait to propose until he was back in good standing with the Church. That meant no popping the question until at least next August, which was well past my deadline. I had to accept that and move forward accordingly.

Today was not about the future, though. Wasn't that what the scriptures said? *Sufficient to the day is the evil thereof.* Today had its own problems and blessings, and I had to take the good with the bad. That meant living every moment to its fullest until my life wasn't my own anymore. It meant having a beautiful night with my dad.

It was after six by the time I returned to his place, refreshed from my day at the spa and in possession of a new dress. I had just under an hour to slip into my new outfit and reapply makeup.

It was seven sharp when I found my dad in the parlor and paused in surprise to see him still in his work clothes.

"I'm shocked," I teased. "I've never known you to be late once in my life."

He looked me over, approval obvious in his eyes. "Oh, my little girl. You look brilliant."

"Thanks, Dad," I said, smiling but confused. "You said seven, right?"

"Yes, and you're right on time." He motioned for me to turn around. The moment he did, I smelled Diesel cologne and knew what I would find behind me . . . or rather, who.

I couldn't speak—couldn't breathe—when I saw Ty waiting for me in the doorway, impeccably dressed in Armani. Luckily, the way he stepped forward and offered me his arm was so natural that reflex alone saved me from being rude. I slipped my arm into his.

"I thought you might enjoy a night on the town with someone more your age." Neither Ty nor I responded, and my dad wisely took it as a cue to disappear, leaving Ty and me to stare at each other.

"You never told me you grew up in a mansion," he finally said.

"You look fantastic," I breathed, not used to seeing him in such high-end clothes.

He cupped my face in his hands and leaned his forehead against mine. "Don't say that. I'm trying really hard to be a gentleman right now by not kissing you in front of your father."

I tilted my chin up and performed the dastardly deed of which he spoke.

"You look stunning," he said, wrapping his arms around me. I hugged him back, caught up in the moment despite myself. *Sufficient to the day is the evil thereof.* Take the good while you can get it!

"What are you doing here?" I whispered more to myself than to him, but he heard me. He kissed my check and whispered back.

"I didn't want you to get used to being alone."

A feeling rippled through me as he said that—one I cannot find the words to describe, but I know without a doubt I will never forget it. Still, I pulled away.

"Ty, I don't know how to explain, but—"

His finger moved to shush me and he smiled. "How about we start with dinner?"

Torn, I decided to relent. "We *are* dressed for it."

"Good choice," he said and led me to the front door.

* * *

I don't know how, but somehow Ty took us all the way through dinner without bringing up our relationship. Instead we spoke of the one thing we had always avoided with each other—our pasts. And when dinner was over, he looked longingly to the beach and asked if I minded taking a walk.

"A stroll on the beach in the moonlight?" I replied. "I think I can deal with that."

Shoes in hand, we walked along in silence. It didn't take a psychic to notice the mood change.

"Why did you run away, Rhea?" he asked softly.

It was the inevitable question, and it deserved a real

answer. "Because I'm a mess, and I don't want to spread that mess around."

He clicked his tongue at me. "Isn't it my decision to decide whether or not I like your mess?"

"Not entirely." I sighed and looked up to the sky. "Things changed in Wyoming, Ty. I mean, I was a stain before, but now it's . . . worse. I have a target on me that can't be erased, and I can't let you live with that."

"And I can't live without you," he returned. "So how else do we deal with this?"

I stopped walking and looked at him. "Don't say that, Ty."

"What? That I love you?"

It felt like someone shot me in the chest with a shotgun, except the shrapnel felt good. I'm not sure what my face looked like at that moment, but I couldn't breathe or couldn't swallow. Only stare.

"You can't tell me you're shocked, Rhea. I've been in love with you since the first day we met in Liberty Park."

I finally managed to inhale. "But you never said it."

"Neither did you," he countered.

"Well no, but—"

"But what?"

I shook my head. "This is no good, Ty. I'm not good at commitment, which is why I liked you. You were accessible but unattainable. You go slow and back away when things get serious. You're safe for me."

He smiled and touched my face. "And I'm still safe, Rhea. I'm not going anywhere just because I'm not afraid to tell you I love you."

I stepped away. "I'm the one who's not safe, Ty. Like I said: things are a little different now."

He nodded. "No doubt about that. I've only known you four months, but I can't handle it when you walk away from me. You do it a lot, if you haven't noticed, and I can't describe the pain I feel when I realize I have no right to chase after you—no claim that will bring you back."

My breath stilled, terrified at the direction he was taking.

"In four months you've claimed my soul, Rhea. Your world is an insane and scary place, but I'm not afraid of it." He gripped my hands with a cautious gentleness. "I'm not afraid of you. I love you."

Terror and elation warred within me. "Did Kay put you up to this?"

He shook his head. "Kay told me not to come. She told me you needed time to think."

"I do," I agreed. "You should have listened to her."

"And leave you alone after all that?" he asked, eyes searching mine. "No one should be alone after what you went through. Kay wouldn't tell me what happened, which, of itself, leads me to believe it was worse than I thought. I want to be the guy to tell you that everything's going to be all right."

He saved me from answering by drawing me against him and holding me tight. It felt like heaven—even though Donald's words hissed in my brain like a taunt.

"I know you want me in your life," he said. "But you never tell me how or to what extent. You leave it to me to figure that part out."

I needed to say something, but my mind was too content to come up with anything off-putting. "And have you?"

"Yes." I didn't move and neither did he.

"And your conclusion?" I asked, just to say something as my hands ran over the familiar shape of him.

"Well, if I just told you, you wouldn't have to pay attention to me, would you?"

I gave him a light swat.

"Kay was right," he mused.

"About what?" I prompted.

"Everything, really, but specifically when she said that you are brilliant at looking into other people's hearts and minds, but have no skill in looking into yourself."

I pulled away, letting him slide my hands into his. "Well, that's nice of her to spread around."

He kissed me softly. "I'll keep your secret. Scout's honor."

I looked away, unable to meet his guileless eyes. He was so good. What was I doing with him?

"My life is too complicated, Ty."

"Rhea, you're not a simple girl, but if you were, I wouldn't love you as much as I do. So it doesn't make much sense for you to use that as an excuse to run away."

Uh-uh. I couldn't be drawn in by that talk. "It's more complicated than that, Ty."

"You've got that right, at least." He dropped to his knee in the sand.

My heart stopped. It literally stopped beating in my chest for a full three seconds, I swear.

My mind screamed for me to stop Ty before he did what we would both surely regret, but instead I looked down at him in mute shock.

"Rhea Abigail Jensen, from the first day I met you I haven't been able to stay away from you. I helped tile your kitchen floor just to talk to you, renovated your basement just to be near you, and helped you landscape your yard for the simple pleasure of watching your skin tan. After going through the hell of seeing you with another man, I vowed never to give you a reason to do that again. And I figure if we can survive the past few days, we're up for pretty much anything."

His eyes were so blue and so earnest in the moonlight. I knew my eyes were shining and I couldn't help but blink a couple of times. Apparently crying was becoming my thing lately.

"I love you, Rhea. I'm happy to be the first to say it, since I'm sure I was the first to feel it. I know you've got all these excuses in your head telling you why you should walk away, but before you do, please know that I don't want you to. Neither of us knows the future, but I know I want you in mine." He reached into his pocket. "That said, I would really love it if you married me."

The moment was surreal. First of all, I had just talked myself into believing this was impossible. Second of all, he had pretty much jumped out of some other girl's fantasy and into my life. I almost laughed. The moonlight, the beach, both of us dressed in formal wear? Other girls must dream of being proposed to just like this only to have the question popped over the Jumbotron at a baseball game.

When he opened the ring box, I gasped.

"Ty, it's huge!"

He blushed. "If you want to trade it in, I'll understand, but let me explain first." He slipped the ring on my finger, making it look like a skinny twig balancing an ice cube. "When it comes to you, I am a jealous man, Rhea. I guess you could say that getting such a large ring serves a selfish purpose for me. I want every man who meets you to be blinded by it, so they know that you are a woman who is loved by a husband who gives you everything he has."

I had no retort for that.

"Rhea, I would do anything in my power to spend forever with you, and after last weekend, I don't want to wait another day for you to know it. I don't ever want you to leave me behind at a diner in Twin Falls again, just because you think you're alone in life. Whatever you need from me, I'll give it to you. All I ask is that you not walk away from that."

His last words dropped me to my knees so I could hug him. "No more," I pled against his suit. "A girl can only take so much."

"Does that mean yes?" he asked, pulling me closer.

"I have a lot to explain to you before I can say that, Ty."

He shook his head. "No, you don't. Right now I'm just looking for the answer that comes from your heart, not your head. In your heart, do you want to marry me?"

I laughed through tears and loved him just a little bit more for his consistent ability to see through me. It seemed so unfair that he had to lay himself out there with a five-minute mono-logue while I got away with a one-word response. But, if it would make him feel half as amazing as I did in that moment, I would give it to him.

I brought my lips to his ear and breathed, "Yes."

He leaned back and looked me in the eye, as if searching to see my agreement echoed there. Looking into each other's eyes from two inches away after agreeing to get married, neither of us fought the urge to lean in and connect. After all, we were just two broken, lovesick fools kneeling on the beach at night, kissing.

"Say it," he whispered.

My mind barely registered his words. "Anything. What?"

He leaned his forehead against mine. "You know."

I leaned in, trying to kiss him again. "I really don't, Ty."

He looked shy and a little disappointed. "I said I didn't mind being the first to say it, but that doesn't mean I'm not in a hurry to hear you say it back."

My heart froze in place and in a flash, my body felt numb. The ocean air suddenly felt cold, and my stomach spun like a top.

Three simple words. That's all he was waiting for. Three words I'd been hiding from him for months. Yet despite all the inner turmoil they had caused me, they were three words I had never gotten around saying at all, except when he was lying asleep on a hotel bed.

I probably should look him in the eye the first time I said them.

"I love you, Ty."

He had been holding his breath. I didn't realize that until it all came out in a whoosh before he once again fused our lips together. It was perfect. He was perfect—for me, at least.

"Ty?"

"Mmm."

"I'll be a very difficult person to be married to."

He kissed the tip of my nose. "I'll make that into a T-shirt you can wear on special days when you're feeling especially dangerous."

It amazed me that under the circumstances, he could still make me laugh.

"But now that we've completed the portion of the evening where we let our hearts do the talking, I'm serious about there being some serious issues you need to know about. We have to talk, Ty," I said, removing the ring and holding it out to him. "And if, when we're done, you still want me to have that, then we'll talk."

"I'm not going—"

I pressed my finger over his lips. "Say that after I'm done talking. Then I'll believe you."

"Fine," he agreed. "But will you put the ring back on?"

I shook my head. "Not until you hear me out. Let's take another walk, shall we?"

Then I told him everything.

SHERALYN PRATT GRADUATED from the University of Utah with a BA in Communication. She loves travel, well-trained dogs, good sushi, and is a sucker for rice krispy treats. To learn more about upcoming projects or to gain insights into the Rhea Jensen series, visit Sheralyn online at www.sheralynpratt.com or follow her on twitter: @sheralynpratt.